Freedom's Whisper

Angela Dorsey

Freedom's Whisper

Original title: Freedom's Whisper
Cover and inside ill: © 2007 Jennifer Bell
Cover layout: Stabenfeldt A/S

Typeset by Roberta L. Melzl
Editor: Bobbie Chase
Printed in Germany, 2007

ISBN: 1-933343-52-4

Stabenfeldt, Inc.
457 North Main Street
Danbury, CT 06811
www.pony.us

The black yearling lifted her head from the verdant spring grasses and pricked her ears toward the trees crowding the far side of her fenced paddock. She snorted and took an elegant step forward, then glanced back to see her dam, Keeta, watching her. The pinto mare nickered and Freedom considered turning back to graze at her dam's side — but something indefinable made her turn toward the forest again.

Freedom walked to the split rail fence and peered into the woody shadows, her blue eyes sharp. The forest looked the same as always: green boughs nodding in the breeze, leaves shimmering, ferns and tiny wildflowers carpeting the forest floor. The subtle whisper and creak of the trees sounded the same as well. A bird flitted past, its wings a flash of striped brown and white. Freedom leaned over the top rail, stretched open her nostrils and inhaled deeply. The forest even smelled as it usually did: both fresh and musky, with a hint of the hot summer sweetness that was soon to come.

Yet even though she couldn't define the difference, Freedom knew something had changed among the trees, something deeper than sound, scent, sight. If only she could reach further than her senses, she might be able to understand. She leaned harder on the fence. Closed her eyes.

"Keeta! Freedom!"

Freedom looked back at the house. Mom was striding across the back lawn with two carrots in her hand. The woman stopped at the fence and held the tempting orange sticks out to the horses. Keeta moved to get her treat, her coat a shimmer of scarlet and ivory.

"Freedom! Carrots!"

The black yearling gazed longingly into the shadows beneath the trees. Mom was a wonderful human, but she'd come along at just the wrong time. The forest was trying to tell Freedom something, something important, but unless she could concentrate, she would never understand its message.

But maybe her human, Jani, could help her. Yes! As soon as Jani was home from that place she went to almost every day — *school*, that was the sound — as soon as she got back, she'd saddle Keeta and halter Freedom, and take them on an outing. Then Freedom could insist they go into the forest. And in the meantime, she might as well have a carrot!

The black yearling spun away from the dark trees and broke into a supple trot. She leapt and bucked the last few yards toward Mom, then stopped short at the fence, her sculpted head held high.

Mom laughed. "You need a trim," she said. "Look at all that hair in your eyes." She held out the carrot and with great dignity, Freedom pulled it from her fingers.

Jani dropped her books on the hall table and hurried through the house toward the back door. She stopped in the kitchen for a moment, to gulp down a glass of water. It was a hot day, one of those lazy, beautiful days that happened in May sometimes. A day that made Jani long for summer vacation. She was halfway through her drink when she registered the scene through the window above the sink, sputtered, coughed, and lowered her glass.

What on earth was her mom doing? Amazed, Jani laughed. Her mom was actually grooming Keeta — not with the right brush, but still, she was grooming the pinto mare. Freedom stood beside them and Jani could see her mom's mouth moving, as if she were talking to the horses. This she had to check out.

"Hi," her mom called as Jani walked across the back lawn.

"I'm shocked, Mom." Jani climbed through the split rail fence. "Since when do you spend time with the horses?"

"I guess it's time to confess," her mom said with a self-conscious smile. "Even though it's not really my fault, since my *only* daughter is too mature to let her poor mother brush her hair for her anymore." She sighed dramatically and turned to slide the soft brush meant for Keeta's face over the mare's sleek side.

"Well, there's not much left to brush on me anymore anyway." Jani ran her fingers through her cropped brown hair. She loved it short. It was so much easier to take care of. And she couldn't help but notice how it made her face look elf-like. Even Penny, her best friend, who begged her not to cut it, admitted that it looked great. Best of all, Mike, who was one grade ahead of Jani and Penny in school, told Bridian last week (who told Penny, who told Jani) that he thought Jani was cute. Jani's face grew hot as she remembered, but thankfully her mom didn't seem to notice she was blushing.

"Here, let me show you how to do it right," Jani offered. She picked the rubber curry from the grooming bucket. "You should start with this one."

Within half an hour, the horses were gleaming, and their long manes and tails slipped like satin through Jani's fingers.

"Are you and Penny going riding in the forest today?" Jani's mom asked, as Jani tightened Keeta's cinch. "Freedom's been pretty antsy to get out, and she keeps staring off into the trees."

Jani stroked the filly's shoulder. "I can't. I already told Penny I'd meet her halfway to the baseball diamond." She patted Keeta's neck before mounting. "We thought it might be good for Freedom to be around crowds a bit."

"Well, it's a nice day to be riding, no matter where you go. Remember to be home in time for supper."

"I will." Jani reined Keeta toward the gate and

Freedom eagerly pranced beside them. They were halfway around the house, close to the trail that dove into the woods, when Freedom stopped short and stared soulfully into the forest. "Not today, Freedom," said Jani and pulled gently on the rope. The filly didn't budge, and Jani pulled again. "Come on, or I'll leave you at home." Freedom hesitated, sighed, then reluctantly obeyed.

Once they were away from the house, Jani asked Keeta to hurry. Because she'd taken the time to explain each grooming tool to her mom, she was late to meet Penny. Keeta broke into a rocking horse canter and Freedom trotted at her side. The wind flowed around them in a warm stream. It really was an amazing spring day.

Ahead of them, Penny rode Sunny around a corner in the road. She loped the bright palomino gelding toward Jani, Keeta, and Freedom.

"Sorry we're late," Jani said, pulling Keeta to a walk.

"I thought maybe you weren't allowed out or something," said Penny, as she turned Sunny around and reined him alongside Keeta. He nickered a greeting to the mare and Keeta pinned her ears back. The girls smiled, and Penny leaned forward to pat the golden neck. "It's heartbreaking, isn't it, Sunny boy? She's so cold and distant, like a spotted ice queen."

"Keeta's not an ice queen," defended Jani.

"Yeah, she likes him fine, as long as he's nowhere near her."

"Well, you have to admit, he's a little obsessed and obvious."

"You mean like Mike?"

Embarrassment colored Jani's face again, but she couldn't stop a small smile from infecting her stern expression.

"Shut up," she said, then laughed. She didn't sound very convincing.

Penny grinned. "Sorry. I know we agreed he was just being *nice* when he called you cute."

"That's right," Jani replied. She knew her ears must be beet red. "And both you and Bridian promised you'd never tell anyone what Mike said. Remember?" A long moment of silence followed her words — uncomfortable silence. She glanced sideways at her friend. "You haven't told anyone, right?"

There was a pause. "Well…"

"Penny! You didn't!" Jani pulled Keeta to a halt, and Penny stopped Sunny beside her.

"Not on purpose. It's just that…"

"What? Tell me what happened?" A feeling of dread was crawling up Jani's spine.

"Remember today in the library when you invited that new girl, Kara, to come to the baseball game with us? Before she walked past us, I was teasing you about Mike, remember?" Penny looked down at her saddle horn and began to trace the stitching with her finger. "Anyway, I didn't realize until she stood up, but she was sitting on the floor *behind* the book cart that was *behind* us. Then she tried to sneak away but you saw her and invited her to come with us because you're so nice, and she totally burned you by not even answering you, which made me mad, and after she was gone I told you how mad I was, and you said you felt sorry for her because she still hasn't made any friends, and..."

"Penny!"

Penny inhaled deeply. "Anyway, I think she was listening to us. And I'm *so* sorry I didn't notice her sitting there earlier, all quiet and reclusive and stuff."

"What exactly did we say?"

"You said that every time you see Mike, you never say the right thing and that he probably thinks you're an idiot," said Penny, sounding as if she were announcing a death. "*And* you said he was cute."

Jani squeezed her eyes shut for a moment. Breathed deep. Tried to collect her thoughts. "Maybe it's a good thing Kara doesn't have any friends yet. She has no one to tell, right?"

Freedom snorted impatiently and bobbed her head, and the two girls asked their horses to walk on.

"I never see her talking to anyone," said Penny.

"So maybe its okay."

"Maybe. I really am sorry, Jani."

"That's okay. I didn't see her either. And honestly, I don't think she'd tell anyone even if she did have friends. There's something about her that seems…"

"Weird?"

Jani laughed. "No. Nice. And *really* shy." Freedom plunged forward, pulling the lead rope taut. "Okay, beauty," Jani said. "Let's go faster."

"Good idea." Penny looked behind them to make sure the country road was still clear, then asked Sunny to lope. Jani, Keeta, and Freedom were right beside them.

Kara opened the front door slowly, quietly. "Sandy?"

No answer.

"Sandy?"

Silence.

Kara walked into the living room. The dirty blanket her mom usually lay under to watch TV flopped on the couch like a giant, mangy cat. Empty coffee cups and dirty plates littered the coffee table. The TV blared.

The kitchen was empty too. Kara opened the fridge door. Some wrinkled apples lay in the bottom drawer of the fridge, and she reached for one, took a bite, then grimaced as she chewed the flesh. It was soft and tasted musty.

She grabbed the ketchup, opened it, and tipped the bottle back. Red ooze squirted into her mouth. She swallowed, glad that the taste of the apple was gone, then squirted some more.

"What are you doing?"

Kara gagged and the ketchup bottle went flying, spraying its contents in red gashes and flecks across the filthy floor.

"You little pig! Is this what I've sacrificed my life for? For you to come home and eat like a disgusting animal?"

Kara couldn't respond, she was coughing so hard. She gulped and gagged, and almost vomited from the force of her spasms.

"You're always eating, eating, eating. Always messing up the house. What do you think I am? Your slave? You think I'm here to clean up after you?" Her mom was standing over her now, legs apart, hands on hips.

"Sorry, Sandy, I'm sorry," Kara sputtered when her air passages were clear. She knew better than to look at her mom's face. She would interpret eye contact as cheekiness, and there would be no way to convince her otherwise. There was nothing Kara could do but stare at the ketchup spreading across the floor, and wait for the verbal barrage to be over.

As if her apology was accepted, there was a sudden silence. Was that it then? Was her mom's anger spent? Kara held her breath, her gaze locked on her mother's worn out sneakers. Slowly, she counted the seconds. Usually it took at least ten. Then her mom would make that final step toward her and wrap her strong arms around her, hug her, and tell Kara that she shouldn't antagonize her like that. She'd say once more that if Kara would just act like a normal child, she would never yell at her. And then Kara would apologize again and again until her mom finally said she forgave her — and everything would be fine once more. Except next time she wouldn't eat straight from the bottle. She usually didn't make the same mistake twice.

Ten seconds came and went. Fifteen. Twenty.

Silence. Thirty seconds. Forty.

"I'm sorry, Sandy, I'm really, really sorry," Kara repeated. The name still seemed stiff on her tongue. Three weeks ago, her mom asked her to call her by her real name, Sandy. She'd said Kara was old enough now to not call her *mom*. Kara hadn't disagreed because she hadn't dared, even though she knew most people called their mothers *mom*, even when they were old. But she hadn't wanted to cause another scene. Her mom was so edgy lately, even though they'd just moved to Red River, and usually she was pretty good after a move. For a few months anyway.

Kara shifted from one foot to the other, looked from her mother's feet to her knees, to her midsection. Her hands were still on her hips. Her bearing was still stiff and unforgiving. What was wrong? Surely, eating from the ketchup bottle wasn't *that* bad, especially when there was nothing else to eat but some musty old apples.

"Mom?" she ventured. "I mean, Sandy, I'm…"

"I can't stand the sight of you!" Her mother spat the words out as if they were cold poison. "You're becoming more and more like her!"

Tears leapt to Kara's eyes, and she gasped and lurched back against the cupboard. Dared to look into her mother's raging eyes.

"You're becoming Marjorie," her mother ranted, a little louder, a little clearer, as if she wanted to be sure every single word assaulted Kara. "I can't stand that you're becoming her!"

Kara's racking sob broke the silence that followed her mother's horrible statement. And then Kara was running.

She slipped on the ketchup as she broke for the door. The next thing she knew, she was outside, racing across the overgrown back lawn. The forest loomed up in front of her, dark and protecting.

"Kara! Come back here right now!" Her mom was calling from the back door. "If you wouldn't do such bad things. If you hadn't spilled the ketchup... But I forgive you. Now get back inside this house!"

At the edge of the forest, Kara paused. Her tears blurred her vision, so she could barely make out her mom standing on the back porch. She'd called Kara *Marjorie* again, whoever that was, but the important thing was that she wanted Kara to come back.

"If you don't come back now..."

The unspoken threat hung in the air between them. Kara almost turned, almost walked back to her mother. Only one thought stopped her. There had been a lot more conviction in the cruel words her mother had spoken in the kitchen than in those she was using to get Kara to return. And now she wasn't saying anything; she was just standing there, watching Kara watch her.

Suddenly, the woman turned and strode back into the house. Kara had left it too long. She lunged into the forest, allowed the trees to engulf her, to hide her passing, as she wove between them with a practiced grace. She knew these woods, and here, only here, she felt safe. In the month she'd lived in Red River, the forest was the one thing she'd allowed herself to become attached to, allowed herself to cherish, and even though it wasn't human or animal, she knew she'd miss it dreadfully when she left.

And she *would* leave. One of these days, she'd come home from school, and her mom would have everything packed into the car, and they'd move on to another town, another city, maybe even another state. Far from Red River. Far from this forest.

A sob burst from her and she slowed, then stopped. She leaned against a large cedar tree and looked up at the massive trunks twisting into the sky around her, reaching for the light. She could understand them. She'd been hoping for some light in her life for a long time: the light of being like every other thirteen-year-old and belonging to a normal family, one that lived in the same house for more than a few months at a time.

And she wanted friends, friends like that girl, Jani, who seemed so nice. She'd known better than to accept Jani's invitation today, no matter how tempted she'd been. Don't get close to anyone — that was the rule.

The last time Kara had a friend was in Grade Two, when she'd met a girl named Camie. The day she got an invitation to Camie's birthday party was one of the happiest of her life. Her first party invitation! But when she told her mom about it, her mom said she couldn't go. Kara tried everything to convince her to change her mind, to no avail. And the next day, when she came home from school, the car was packed. Before they left, her mom explained that this move was *her* fault, that if she hadn't made friends with Camie, they wouldn't be moving.

Kara stopped making friends after that. In fact, she wasn't even sure she knew how to anymore. Jani's had been the first invitation she'd received in a long, long time, and Kara knew she'd been rude to her. She'd just been so surprised at being noticed, let alone being invited somewhere, that she hadn't known how to respond.

Kara slid down the rough bark to settle on the soft moss. Tears streamed down her cheeks. Here she could cry as much as she wanted and there was no one to hear. Here she didn't have the added ache of crying silently.

What was she going to do? Her mother hated her. And it was all her own fault. If Kara could just do the right things, or at least avoid doing wrong things, everything would be fine. But she couldn't seem to stop herself from constantly hurting the one and only person who loved her — her mother. Kara sniffled and wiped her nose.

But still, how it hurt to hear those terrible words! Even knowing she might deserve it didn't lessen the sting. Kara bit her lip and covered her head with her hands. Silent screams vibrated through her skull. How did one change who they were inside? She would do it in an instant, if she knew how. Maybe change into someone like Jani. Surely Jani's mom loved her.

A twig snapped. Kara's sense of preservation made her hold her breath and listen. Was it just a small branch falling from a tree? Or a wild animal? A *bear*? She'd heard there were black bears in this forest, though she'd never seen one.

Kara had almost decided it was nothing, when another twig snapped. And again, even closer. Something was walking toward her! Slowly she stood, careful not to make a sound, and peered through the trees. The creature was not small, of that she was certain, because it was breaking twigs regularly. She searched for a climbable tree, and when she found one with low branches a few yards to her right, she looked back in the direction of the sounds. Tried to calm down. Tried to think. She was probably jumping to conclusions on the bear idea. The noise could mean a deer or a moose too. Kara exhaled silently. In fact, it probably was a deer. Deer were way more plentiful in the forest than bears. And wouldn't it be wonderful if a deer walked near her?

The branches parted and Kara's breath caught in her chest. There it was. Not a deer. Not a bear. Not a moose. A beautiful vision, a glorious creature — an ethereal white foal! And it had just stepped into a single spot of sunlight, only ten yards away from her. It froze, looking as elegant and sculpted as a timeless masterpiece, sniffed the air warily and swiveled its delicate ears toward her. Kara didn't realize she'd moved, putting her hand to her mouth in awe, until the foal was leaping and bounding away.

"Wait for me!" Kara yelled. She darted after the foal. When it disappeared in the undergrowth, she followed its sound the best she could. As the crackling noises became more distant, Kara had to keep stopping to listen so she'd know which way to go.

Finally, she broke off her pursuit at a huge fir tree. She knew her way home from here, but no farther. The last shreds of sound from the foal's passing faded and silence reigned in the forest once more.

Kara sank into the soft moss again and leaned back against thick rutted bark. But this time she didn't weep. This time a dreamy smile lingered upon her face. She'd

seen a unicorn, one too young to have a horn yet, though she'd seen where the horn would grow. There'd been a single dark spot on the top of the foal's head, between its ears.

And because of this magical experience, she was different inside. There was a spark of fire in her heart now, glowing as beautifully as the unicorn foal in its spot of sunlight. Kara knew she would never feel the same — about the forest, about life, about herself — ever again. She might be a terrible person, so terrible that even her own mother loved her less and less every day, but this one thing about her was *beyond* good. There was one precious, special thing about her after all. She'd seen a baby unicorn!

Freedom pawed the floor of her stall and snorted. Jani had put her in the barn that night, even though Freedom had made it clear she wanted to stay outside. She'd hoped that at night, with her vision limited, she might be able to glean more information from the forest. But no. Jani put Keeta and Freedom into their stalls, fed and groomed them well, then went off to her own barn.

Freedom tried to sleep for a long time. Tried to not pace. She listened to Keeta breathing steadily in the stall next to hers, and then to the subtle sounds in the barn as the wind picked up. When the rain started, all was drowned out by the torrents descending on the tin roof. She dozed then, just a bit, but when the rain stopped, the new silence woke her — and she could once again feel the forest's strange ambience, like a living thing whispering to her from far away.

The yearling bent her head over her stall door and eyed the door latch in the early morning light. If only she could figure out the contraption that held her stall door shut. She'd seen Jani unlatch it countless times. Surely, she too could open it. And then she could go to the window across the barn, the one that was open, and smell the night air. That, at least, would be something.

Her muzzle brushed against metal, pushed this way, that way. But the door didn't open. She pressed down on the latch. Again, harder — too hard. That hurt! Freedom snorted, and eyed her small, shiny jailer with pinned ears. Then one ear flickered forward. Maybe if she pulled upward on the moving part? She reached down and parted her teeth, gingerly took hold of the metal, and raised it slowly. The door swung outward. She was free! She strode into the barn aisle.

Instantly, Keeta was on her hooves, nickering over her stall door. *Are you okay? What's wrong? What happened? What are you doing?*

Freedom stopped to nuzzle her dam. *I'm okay. Nothing's wrong. Trust me.* Then she continued to the window. Halfway there, she stopped and turned. Maybe she could open the barn door too. That would be the best, because then she could go outside. Then she could go to the forest edge!

She tried pushing, pulling, and moving the contraption side to side on the main doors, but nothing seemed to work. All the metal parts seemed frozen into place, unlike the latch on her stall. Or maybe she just wasn't doing it right. She stood back and stared at it. It looked different than the stall latch. And she was wasting time. She could listen to the trees from the window.

Her muzzle wouldn't fit in the small crack created by the open window, so Freedom pressed her nostrils to the opening. She inhaled, cautiously at first, then deeply. Closed her eyes. Yes, she could sense something different. Minutes passed as she concentrated. Half an hour. In her head, she could see the trees' shadowy forms reaching for the sky, eternally occupied in their ancient creak and sway. But they weren't completely oblivious to those that wandered among them. They had sensed something unusual in their midst. Something that had disturbed them. But what?

With great respect, Freedom presented the question to them. And as was the way of the forest, the answer came slowly, like sap oozing from a wounded tree. Again in her mind's eyes, Freedom saw a shapeless form moving among them, small, alone, and frightened. A creature that needed help. Her help.

She snorted softly to the being, hoping that somehow her compassion would carry to the poor thing, for this soul was lost. This one was not where it should be.

Her snort roused Keeta again, and the mare nickered behind her. *It is almost time for Jani.* Reluctantly, Freedom turned. Her dam was right, and she didn't want to be caught outside her stall. She stepped into the enclosure, turned, and bumped the door with her chin, then backed so it would swing shut. The latch caught.

Freedom yawned. She was tired — but should she rest? She needed to discover who this creature was and why it was lost. She needed to think of what she could do to help it.

Her eyes drooped and she inhaled deeply. After the concentration needed to hear the trees, she felt muddled and unfocused. Slowly, her head lowered. With a little rest, her mind would be clearer. Then, when morning fully arrived, she would think of some way to convince Jani to take her into the forest.

Jani and Penny rode their horses single file along the sun-dappled woodland trail. The thud of hooves made a merry sound, especially with Freedom cavorting and prancing before them.

"I can't wait until school's out." Jani sighed. "Then every day can be like today."

Penny smiled, and turned on Sunny's back to look at Jani and Keeta. "Me too. I don't think I can take another stuffy history lesson." When Keeta nickered, Penny added, "Keeta's saying, *me three.*"

"She gets pretty bored hanging out in the pasture all day. Good thing she has Freedom to keep her company. Otherwise, she'd die of boredom."

"Sunny would go nuts if he was an only horse," said Penny. "I think he might even have a new girlfriend at his stables. Her name's Mystic."

"That's a pretty name. What's she like?" asked Jani.

"She's as pretty as her name," said Penny. "You should come see her tomorrow."

"I'd love to," said Jani, then frowned. "Hey, Freedom's going the wrong way." The filly had turned down the left fork of a Y in the trail. Jani nudged Keeta into a fast walk. Sunny nickered at the mare as she passed, and Keeta laid her ears back at him. Her eyes flashed warningly.

Sunny sighed and his head drooped. "I still love you, boy," murmured Penny, reaching to straighten the palomino's creamy mane. "And so does Mystic."

"Freedom!" Jani called. The filly had disappeared around a corner in the trail.

"Its okay, Jani," said Penny. "We don't have to go the lake. It's cool enough riding in the shade."

Jani stopped Keeta and looked back. "You sure you don't mind?"

"I love playing 'Follow the Filly.' Let's see where she takes us."

Freedom strode down the well-worn trail for a half mile, then chose another obscure trail to the right. Jani and Penny chatted happily as they rode behind her. This was a trail they'd only taken once and they'd never gotten to the end of it. After following Freedom for another half mile, Jani remembered why. It was brushy and overgrown, becoming rougher the farther they traveled. She was spending half her time crouched over Keeta's neck, avoiding being swept off by branches. After another hundred yards, she pulled the mare to a halt. "That's enough for me. I want to do some galloping today, and not spend all my time bushwhacking."

Penny looked ready to turn around as well. Twigs and leaves were stuck in her long hair.

Jani slid from Keeta's back and grabbed the lead rope that was looped around the saddle horn. She held

Keeta's reins out for Penny to hold. "Just let me get Miss Adventure. I don't want her taking off down another trail."

Freedom was waiting for them around yet another bend in the overgrown path, and when she saw Jani approaching, she whinnied to her, then continued to walk.

"Wait, Freedom!" Jani called and broke into a jog behind the yearling. Her hand slid along the black's hindquarters, then her side, and finally she grabbed Freedom's halter. "Whoa, beauty," she murmured. "What's gotten into you today?" She clipped the rope to Freedom's halter, and turned to go — but then hesitated. Something had captured Freedom's attention. She was staring intently into a thicket just a few yards from the trail.

Jani's heart raced. Was something hiding in the bushes? She gathered her courage and called out, "Who's there?"

There was no response. Not even a rustle of leaves. Jani picked up a pinecone and lobbed it toward the mass of vegetation. Still nothing.

"Come on, Freedom," she said, the hairs on the back of her neck prickling. "Let's get out of here."

Kara walked across the overgrown lawn toward her back door, her head hanging in defeat and exhaustion. She hadn't found the unicorn, though she'd been searching all day. The only good thing that had happened was that Jani hadn't seen her in the thicket. What a shock that had been — hearing something approach, wondering if it was a wild animal or the unicorn, and deciding to hide just in case. And then hearing Jani's voice call, "Who's there?" What would Jani have thought of her if she found her cowering in the bushes? That would've been beyond embarrassing.

Now, if she could just get up to her room without seeing her mom, she could fall into bed and rest. Otherwise... well, either her mom would yell at her for not staying home so they could spend their usual Saturday together, or worse, she would look blankly at Kara and turn away, continuing to give her the silent treatment.

Usually Kara spent weekends sitting in front of the TV with her mom, listening to her comment on the characters in the different shows, and occasionally getting snacks from the food cupboard her mom kept locked most of the time. When Kara was little, she'd been bored by the adult shows they'd watch, but she loved the snacks and curling up next to her mom, especially on cold winter days. It had made her feel cozy and safe.

But now it was becoming harder to sit and do nothing, and unpleasant too, since her mom seemed mad at her most of the time. Every weekend it was a little more difficult to sit and stare mindlessly at a TV screen while the entire world lay outside their door. At one time, she'd tried to interest her mom in doing something different — in going swimming, or hiking, or just sitting out in the backyard to listen to the birds — but the harder she tried, the more irritable her mother became. So Kara swallowed her frustration and sat on the couch and pretended to be interested.

Now everything was different. She'd seen the unicorn and there was no way she was going to waste *this* weekend in front of the TV. Sitting, doing nothing, while the unicorn foal might be waiting for her outside? Impossible!

Kara swallowed nervously as she approached the dark house, then gave a sigh of relief. There it was: the faint light of the TV flickering from the living room window. Good. She crept to the dirty glass and peered inside. There was her mom, lying on the couch, her hand moving from the popcorn bowl to her mouth, methodically, robotically, over and over. The lights were off, and the glow of the TV flickered over her mother's face, reflecting in her mesmerized eyes.

Kara shuddered. She'd never realized before what a creepy scene this was. The sight was so familiar that

she'd never thought about it before, but her mom looked like a zombie. For a moment, she wondered if Jani's parents watched so much TV, but then she firmly pushed the thought from her mind. It made her feel disloyal.

And there was one good thing about her mom being so engrossed in her show. Kara could go in through the back door and up to her room without being noticed. In the morning, she'd leave early, before her mom woke up to watch her Sunday morning shows. Kara wasn't about to give up on finding the unicorn yet and she couldn't wait until next weekend; it could be miles away by then. If it wasn't already.

Jani hurried across the back lawn. The horses would be hungry. She was late to feed them this morning, not because she'd slept in, but because her aunt had phoned, specifically to talk to her. Apparently she wanted insight into the teenaged mind to help her with her son Cody, Jani's older cousin.

As if I can understand big teenagers, Jani mused. *If she asked about horses, I could answer that. But seventeen year olds? I don't think so.*

As she hurried toward the barn, Jani's gaze went automatically to the mass of wildflowers in the corner of the pasture. A year and a half ago, the old barn had stood there, dark and foreboding. Jani's heart quickened. The memory of walking into that barn and seeing Freedom for the first time, back when her loving filly had been a wild, hate-filled spirit, still frightened her. Somehow, against all odds, they'd made friends. Then she and Penny had freed the amazing ghost from her prison, by burning the barn to the ground.

But that wasn't the memory that thrilled Jani the most. The most amazing thing happened the next spring, when Keeta gave birth to a foal that was obviously the wild spirit, returned. Jani still didn't understand how the miracle of Freedom's birth could have happened. Even though a year had passed, the filly's mysterious sire had never been found. No wonder Freedom seemed unlike any horse she'd ever known.

Jani flung the door wide and hurried to Freedom's stall. "How are you, little girl?" she said to the black, even though the filly was anything but small. Jani made a mental note to measure Freedom again soon. She looked almost 14.3 hands tall now, big for a yearling.

Freedom nickered and leaned over the stall door, her blue eyes bright with anticipation. Jani stroked her neck. "Good morning to you too," she said, and rested her cheek on Freedom's forehead for a moment before continuing.

She stopped at Keeta's stall on the way to the feed room. "Good morning, Keeta." She smiled when the mare nickered back to her. "I'm fine. How are you today?" The mare nickered again and stepped close, nuzzled the girl's cheek. "I totally agree. It is a lovely morning," Jani answered. She gently pulled two straw stalks from Keeta's forelock, then rubbed the mare on her velvet nose.

In the feed room, Jani measured out the oats, added a spoonful of vitamins to each bucket, stirred, and carried the morning grain back toward the eager horses. The sound of rustling oats and chewing filled the small barn. With a contented sigh, Jani carried the grooming bucket into Keeta's stall. The mare had a manure stain on of one of her white patches, and Jani briskly removed as much of the discoloration as she could, then leisurely continued grooming. When the mare shone a glistening red and white in the low light of the stable, she moved on to Freedom.

"At least you're black and poop stains don't show on you," Jani said as she stepped into the second stall. She set the grooming bucket on the floor, leaned on the filly's side, and inhaled deeply. How she loved weekend mornings. They were so relaxed compared to school mornings. She could linger as long as she wanted. Except for the chores her parents gave her, her entire day was her own. "But really, I should say that you're *almost* all black," she added, dreamily. Her fingers found the small star-shaped patch on Freedom's chest and traced the white edge. The unusual spot was yet another thing that was extremely cool about the young horse.

"Jani!" Her dad's voice came from far away.

Jani sighed and closed her eyes. "What now?"

"Jani!"

"I told him I'd do dishes after I took care of you guys," she grumbled. Didn't he have any work to do at the newspaper office?

"Jani!"

But wait. Her dad didn't sound irritated. He sounded anxious. Maybe something was wrong.

"Be right back," Jani whispered and patted Freedom's shoulder. At the barn door, she stopped. Her dad was standing on the back porch. "I'm here," she called out. "In the barn."

He hurried across the lawn toward the paddock fence, the wireless phone in his hand. "It's Penny. Something's wrong. She's crying."

Jani ran to the fence. "What happened? Did she say anything?"

Her dad shook his head, his face worried. "She's not making much sense, and besides, she asked for you. I didn't want to pry."

Jani grabbed the receiver. "Penny? What's wrong?" She glanced back. Her dad was walking toward the house, but slowly, as if he wanted to know what was happening but didn't want to intrude.

"He's gone! I can't…" Penny's words were broken by a sob. "I can't find him anywhere!"

"Who is? Who's gone?" Jani asked, completely forgetting her dad.

"Sunny!"

"What do you mean, *gone*? How can he be gone? Where are you?"

"At the… the stable."

"I'll be right there, okay?"

"Hurry."

"I will." Jani clicked the phone off. Her father had turned around, and was waiting for her to speak. "Dad? Can you take me to Evergreen Stables?" Her words tumbled over one another in a rush. "Sunny's missing. Can we go right now?"

"What happened?"

"I'll tell you everything I know in the car." Jani climbed through the fence and ran toward the garage.

"Wait, Jani!" When she stopped, he continued in an agonizingly slow tone. "Here, bring me the phone, and try to calm down. You're not going to make things any better for Penny if you're panicking too."

Jani breathed deeply and tried to collect her thoughts. Her dad was right. The best way to help Penny would be to calmly suggest ways to find Sunny. He couldn't have gone far. He wouldn't leave all his horse buddies at the stable, unless some of them had gone missing too. But even if that was the case, what could happen to them? At the worst, they were probably trampling people's gardens.

"I'll go get my keys and wallet, and meet you at the car in two minutes, okay?" her dad continued, his voice even and patient.

"Okay. I have to turn Freedom and Keeta out before we go anyway."

The moment Jani turned Freedom loose, the yearling trotted to the gate, wheeled around, and looked at Jani with piercing eyes. Jani turned back to Keeta. "You take good care of your bored daughter, okay?" she whispered to the mare, and quickly hugged her.

When she reached Freedom, she gave the filly a quick hug as well. "Sorry, beauty," she said. "Sunny's gone and I have to help Penny find him. I'll take you out later today, when I get home, okay?"

Jani climbed through the fence and ran toward the garage, but when she reached the corner, she heard a shrill neigh. She stopped and looked back. Keeta was grazing peacefully, but Freedom was still standing at the gate, staring after Jani with a peculiar look in her icy eyes. A trickle ran down Jani's spine. Freedom was acting as if she knew something was wrong, maybe even *what* was wrong. But how could she?

Frustrated, Jani shook her head. Freedom was an extremely unusual horse, of that she had no doubt, but the filly wasn't *that* different from normal horses. She couldn't know that Sunny was missing from his stable, almost two miles away. Could she?

Penny was almost hysterical when Jani arrived at the stable. She burst into fresh tears the moment she saw Jani and her father hurrying toward her. Mr. Regan, the stable owner, seemed relieved that someone else had arrived to take Penny off his hands and muttered something about going to give the stabled horses their grain.

Jani sat beside Penny on a bale of straw. "So tell me what happened," she said in as calm a voice as she could muster. If her dad could be composed and unflustered, then so could she.

"I had a dream last night…" Penny stopped to wipe away her tears. Stable dirt from her hands streaked across her cheeks. "It was about Sunny, and I kept hearing him neighing, but I couldn't find him. There was all this fog, and I kept calling his name and his neighs kept getting farther and farther away. It was terrible."

Jani's dad handed Penny a handkerchief. She accepted it gratefully and smeared away her fresh tears, taking most of the dirt with it.

"And so you phoned Mr. Regan as soon as you got up?" Jani guessed.

Penny nodded. "He said he was sure everything was fine, but that he'd go check anyway." She sounded completely miserable as she continued. "He called back to say that both Sunny and Mystic were gone, and that either the catch on their gate malfunctioned or someone pulled a prank and let them out." She paused to sniffle. "But he was sure they wouldn't go far. I rode my bike over and started to look for them. I followed their tracks, but then they got on the road and the tracks disappeared." Penny sobbed again. "And Mr. Regan can't find them either. He's going out searching again as soon as the rest of the horses are fed. He sent the new stable hand, Robbie, out to search too."

"We'll help look too, right, Dad?" Jani asked, looking up at her father with a pleading look on her face. "You can drive us around, right?"

"Of course. We'll check all the roads nearby and drive past all the farmer's fields, just in case they stopped in somewhere for breakfast."

"Thanks so much, Mr. Preston!" Penny blurted. "I asked Mom if she could help, and she said as soon as she finds a babysitter for the boys, but she's been trying and can't find anyone. Everyone's busy this weekend. And my dad's out of town right now." She jumped to her feet, wringing her hands in front of her. "I don't know how to say thanks enough. You saved my life, and maybe Sunny's too. I wish I could tell you…"

"Come on, let's get going," interrupted Jani. She knew her friend well enough to recognize that Penny's babbling was a sign of stress. The best thing they could do for her would be to start looking for Sunny.

"Show us where the tracks ended," Jani's dad

suggested. "We can start there and continue on in the direction the horses were traveling."

They drove the back roads for hours, slowly moving farther and farther from the stable. They peered into all the farmer's fields and barnyards, and even knocked on doors when someone was home. But no matter how carefully they looked, they didn't see the flash of gold that would signify Sunny, or the dappled gray that meant Mystic. It was as if the two horses had disappeared off the face of the earth.

Finally, about one o'clock in the afternoon, Jani's dad regrettably told them that he had to go to work at the newspaper office. He dropped the girls off at home after telling them he'd have time to continue the search that evening.

Jani and Penny flopped down on the couch in the living room. "I just don't understand it," Penny whispered. "Where could they go? It's as if they suddenly decided to take a cross country hike or something."

Jani leaned back on the soft fabric and closed her eyes. "We just have to think of more places. I mean, they have to be somewhere," she said, trying to counteract Penny's despair. "Maybe they're hiding, not on purpose, but maybe they found some great grazing in a gully or some other place where we can't see them from the road."

"Maybe." Penny sounded like she was battling tears again.

"Or hey, I know." Jani sat up. "Maybe someone found them and realized they weren't safe wandering about, and put them in their corral or barn."

Penny jumped up. "We should phone the animal shelter! Maybe someone's reported finding them."

"Good idea!" Jani jerked the phonebook out of the drawer and flipped to the correct page. Penny clutched the receiver as Jani dialed, but when the phone started to ring, she thrust the receiver toward Jani. "Can you?" she choked.

"Sure." Jani waited for someone to answer, and when they did, her words came in a rush. "Hi, we were wondering if anyone reported finding some stray horses? We're missing some. Two actually."

"One moment please," the receptionist said. Jani tapped her foot impatiently as they waited, and Penny stood with her arms wrapped tight around her body, a pained expression on her face.

"Hello?" A different voice. "You're calling about missing horses? Are these the two that got out from a paddock at Evergreen Stables this morning?"

"Yes," blurted Jani. "Did someone find them?" Beside her, Penny's face lit up with hope.

"No, not yet. But Mr. Regan is already in contact with us. We'll call him if anyone reports them."

"Okay, thanks," Jani said dejectedly, and disconnected. She looked at Penny, and sighed. "No luck." Tears brimmed in Penny's eyes. "But we can keep looking on our own," Jani added quickly. "We can ride Keeta, and check out some of the places that cars can't go."

Penny nodded, too emotional to speak.

"Come on," said Jani. "There's no point in hanging around here, wasting time." She led the way out the back door. Within minutes, Keeta was saddled and ready.

Jani held the gate open as Penny led the mare through, then shut it quickly before Freedom could follow. When Penny looked at her curiously, she explained that they could cover more ground if they didn't have to lead Freedom.

"Good idea," agreed Penny. She swung into the western saddle, then slid back behind the cantle, and leaned back to let Jani mount.

"We'll be back as soon as we can, Freedom," said Jani, though she knew it wouldn't console the filly at all. She was going to hate being left behind. She asked Keeta to walk on, and glanced back only when a loud neigh came from behind them.

Freedom was still standing at the gate, but now she was striking the ground, hard. As Jani watched, the filly stretched her head in the air and neighed again. The sound boomed around them. And then Freedom was pawing the ground again, over and over.

The image of Freedom pawing the ground by the big rock, back when she was a wild spirit, shoved its way into Jani's mind. Freedom had been striking the ground to tell Jani something then, something important. Could she be doing the same thing now?

"Let's go," Penny said behind her, her voice infinitely sad.

I don't have time now, but when I get home tonight, I'll try to figure it out, thought Jani. *If there is anything to figure out.*

"Walk on, Keeta," she said aloud, and urged the mare forward.

Freedom waited for the sound of Keeta's hooves to fade in the distance, just in case her girl changed her mind and came back for her. Jani was obviously distressed, and Penny even more upset. What could be wrong? Whatever it was, it had to be important. Jani wouldn't ignore her for no reason.

When the soft noise changed to silence, she turned to the gate. It was time to act. Keeta, Jani, and Penny could be gone for hours, and even when they came home, they probably wouldn't take Freedom into the forest. They'd be tired from their outing.

No, her hope lay in her own actions now. Full of determined resolve, Freedom took the gate latch in her teeth.

Kara was tired. She'd wandered the forest for hours, and seen nothing. Finally, in desperation, she walked back to the spot where she'd first seen the unicorn. She searched the ground, looking for anything unusual, even though it had been a day and a half now since she'd seen the foal.

She carefully brushed leaves aside and peered at old indentations. Were one of these marks from the unicorn's hooves? Or was he heavy enough to even imprint the ground? Maybe the magic of unicorns kept them lighter than horses and he made no marks at all. She didn't know much about unicorn lore, unfortunately, and of course a trip to the library was out of the question. There was no way she'd be allowed to go.

Finally, Kara straightened. Maybe there was nothing she could do but wait for the magical creature to reappear. But why would it? It had been so frightened of her and it had no reason to return. There was nothing special about her, other than the fact she'd once seen it.

Maybe she should just give up and go home. It would probably be smart to admit that the baby unicorn was lost to her forever. And yet she knew she had to continue her hopeless search, for one simple reason — she couldn't bear the thought of never seeing *her* unicorn ever again.

Jani and Penny rode Keeta down every back road they could think of, searching for signs of Sunny and Mystic. They rode into every farm and pasture with an open gate that the horses might have slipped through. For hours they searched, talked to people, and called Sunny, but they didn't come across a single sign of the two wayward horses.

When they had exhausted all the *tame-lands*, as Penny liked to call them, they rode into the *wild-lands* — forests and foothills — but here too, they had no luck. They traversed trail after trail, circumnavigated every lake they came across, called for Sunny until their throats were hoarse, but heard and saw nothing that might mean the horses had gone that way. Finally, at the base of a steep hill, Jani pulled a sweating Keeta to a stop. "She needs a rest," she explained to Penny.

Penny slid from the mare's back, and moved to Keeta's head. The horse was breathing heavily. "I'm sorry to make you work so hard, Keeta," she whispered. She pulled a crumbling oatmeal cookie from her pocket. "And I really love you for helping us find Sunny." The mare nickered in return and delicately removed the offered cookie from Penny's fingers. The girl blinked back tears as she stroked Keeta's cheek.

"We'll find him, Penny." Jani didn't know what else to say.

Penny blinked even harder and turned away. Jani sighed as her friend walked toward a big fir tree and sat beneath it, her head in her hands. She could totally imagine how horrible Penny must feel — the same way she would feel if Freedom or Keeta went missing. It would be almost unbearable.

Quickly, she loosened Keeta's girth, so the mare would be more comfortable during her rest, unhooked one side of the single long rein from Keeta's bridle, and sat beside Penny.

The girls sat in companionable silence as Keeta's head drifted lower and her eyelids drooped. She wasn't even searching for grass or other edibles, Jani noticed. The mare must be *very* tired. And no wonder. It was already late afternoon. They'd been riding for hours. Soon they'd have to go back home and check in with her mom and dad.

"Hey Penny, how about we head back and phone Mr. Regan," Jani suggested. "Maybe they've found the horses."

Penny's hopeful gaze met Jani's. "Do you think there's a chance?" she asked.

"I'm sure Mr. Regan and Robbie kept on looking, and Mr. Regan might have even found some other people to help. I think it's worth a shot."

"More than anything, I hope we're not doing all this for nothing," said Penny, as she climbed to her feet. "As long as Sunny is back in his stall, munching oats and wondering where the heck I am!"

47

Jani smiled. "He's probably mad at you for not visiting him yet today." She tightened Keeta's cinch again. "Sorry, girl," she said when the mare groaned dramatically. "Its downhill all the way home, and when you get there, I'll give you some extra oats."

It took them almost an hour to get home. At the front of the house, the girls dismounted, and Penny ran inside to phone Mr. Regan. Jani led Keeta around the house toward the pasture. When the pasture came into view, Jani's heart lurched wildly in her chest. She stopped short. Keeta halted abruptly behind her. A loud snort burst from the mare. The pasture gate was hanging open!

Jani's eyes swept the paddock. No Freedom in sight! She ran toward the open gate with Keeta trotting behind her. Maybe the filly was in the barn. But even as she ran toward the new building, Jani knew Freedom wouldn't be there. Not with the gate open. Not when she'd so desperately wanted to follow them.

But I double-checked the latch, Jani thought. *I remember because I was thinking of how Sunny and Mystic escaped.*

So how had Freedom gotten out? Had she learned to undo the latch? Or was someone targeting Jani and Penny's horses? But they had no enemies, or none she could think of. That girl, Kara, was a little strange, but she didn't seem malicious or anything.

A sudden, horrible thought leapt into Jani's head, making her heart thud even faster. No! That was just a crazy idea! The horses couldn't have been stolen, could they?

But there had been no signs of Sunny and Mystic all day and that was incredibly unusual. And for Freedom to 'accidentally' get out as well was too much of a coincidence. Jani felt her mouth drop open in shock. Could that be the answer to their mystery? Could professional horse thieves have come to Red River?

"They haven't found them yet, and no one's called from the animal shelter either." Penny's dejected voice came from behind Jani.

Slowly Jani turned to face her friend.

"Jani? What's wrong? You look like you've seen a ghost." Their old running joke, the one they'd had since Freedom came into their lives, but this time Jani knew Penny wasn't trying to be funny.

Jani could barely force herself to say the words. They made everything seem so dreadfully final. But somehow she pushed them out. "Freedom's gone too."

Penny's gaze turned to the pasture. "But how? We latched the gate. I even double checked it."

"Me too, and it was latched right."

"But then, how did she get out?" A gasp. "No! You think someone opened it. Someone turned her loose."

"Or someone stole her. And maybe Sunny and Mystic too." It was all Jani could say before misery choked her into silence.

"We're phoning the police, right now," Penny exclaimed. She took Keeta's reins from Jani's hand and tied the mare to the fence, then put her arm around her friend and led her toward the house. "Maybe Freedom,

Sunny, and Mystic aren't the only horses missing. Maybe others have disappeared too."

"They might already have some leads," Jani sputtered hopefully. She brushed away the tears on her cheeks, and straightened her back as they climbed the stairs to the back door. She couldn't despair, not yet. There was too much to do, and it wasn't fair to Penny. Sunny was missing too. How could she expect Penny to be the only strong one?

She grabbed the phone book and found the number, then read it aloud as Penny dialed. While the call was connecting, she ran to her parent's bedroom and picked up the phone by their bed. A police officer had just answered their call and Penny was explaining the situation to him.

"Hold on," he said, when Penny finished. "That's Officer Hughes' department. I'll transfer you."

Silence as they waited.

"Hello. Officer Hughes here. How can I help you?"

"Hi. We were wondering if any horses have been reported missing lately." Penny's voice was shrill. "Ours are gone and we can't find them anywhere, and we wondered if maybe more horses might be missing, which might mean someone's stealing them."

"Actually, there is speculation that a horse thief *might* be working in this area, but no proof. Five horses have gone missing over the last week, all from nearby towns and all from explainable causes."

"What do you mean?"

"One had a tree fall and break down her fence, and a

mare and foal got out when the battery on their electric fence went dead, and the other two got out when their barn door wasn't latched properly. Can you tell me what happened with your horses?"

"It was the same kind of thing: latches on gates coming undone," explained Penny. "But we're not sure if Sunny and Mystic's paddock was latched right."

"But Freedom was in a different paddock and we latched that one right, for sure," added Jani, finally speaking up. "We double checked it, both of us. And we've been searching all day for Sunny and Mystic, and it's like they just disappeared. There are no tracks or horse poop or anything."

"Where are they being stabled?"

"Sunny and Mystic are — were — at Evergreen Stables, out on Bay Road. The owner is Mr. Regan. And Freedom was at the Preston's on Solomon Way," said Penny.

"We just barely found out she's missing," said Jani. "We were out looking for the others." Hot tears were forming and her throat hurt.

"Can you give me a quick description?"

"Sunny's a palomino gelding with a blaze and four socks," said Penny. "And Mystic is a dapple gray Andalusian mare. Freedom's a black yearling filly with a small white spot on her chest and blue eyes."

"Wow. That'll be a distinctive one. Not what thieves usually go for," said Officer Hughes.

"What do you mean?" Jani managed to ask.

"Usually horse thieves choose horses that are more common colors. Even a palomino might be taking a chance that the horse is too recognizable," explained the police officer. "Okay, I'll tell you what I'll do. I'll drive out and talk to Mr. Regan, and have a look around the stables. I'll need your names, addresses, and phone numbers too, in case I have more questions, and I'll call before I come out to the Preston's to make sure you're there."

As Penny gave him the information, Jani gently hung up the phone. She had to think. Of course they would take Keeta and go out searching again, even if the mare was exhausted. It was still remotely possible that the missing horses *hadn't* been stolen, in which case Jani and Penny needed to keep looking.

A rush of guilt discolored Jani's thoughts. If only she'd thought of the thief thing earlier, then she would've brought Freedom with them as they searched. Freedom had wanted to come too, which made her feel even worse. But instead of opening the gate, instead of putting the halter and lead rope on the filly, Jani had turned her back on the young horse and ridden away. She'd let Freedom down. The black's disappearance was all her fault. If she'd just listened...

But she had to get a grip. Reproaching herself now would only waste time, and it certainly wouldn't help Freedom. There was only one thing to do if she was smart — put all her feelings of guilt aside, or as much as possible anyway. When Freedom was safely back in her paddock, then Jani could be angry at herself. Then she could tell herself, with as much vehemence as she wanted, how completely and utterly horrible she was.

"Whoa, Keeta." The pinto mare stopped and her ears flicked back, listening. "She needs another rest," said Jani. Stiffly, Penny dismounted and Jani followed her. Keeta groaned as Jani loosened the cinch, then shook like a soaked dog. Sweat droplets went flying, but neither girl complained. They were both too tired for that.

Penny slumped down on the forest floor and put her head in her hands. "Do you think we'll find them, Jani?" she asked quietly.

"Yes," Jani said, her voice overly loud in the forest silence. But it had to be true. The alternative was too horrible to think about.

Keeta neighed stridently and Jani jumped at the sudden sound. The mare's head was up and her ears were taut forward. She stared off into a thick mass of bushes.

Penny was on her feet in an instant. "Sunny?" she called. "Sunny, boy! Cookie! Come get your cookie!"

Twigs crunched underfoot as Keeta walked toward the bushes. Jani hurried beside her, leaning forward to peer into the shadowy depths of the thicket. "Freedom! Come, Freedom. Time to go home," she called, a hopeful lilt to her voice.

A slight rustling came from the thicket. Then silence.

"It's a squirrel," said Penny.

Jani shook her head. "Keeta wouldn't care about a squirrel," she whispered, and put her finger to her lips. She handed the mare's reins to Penny, and then silently, stealthily, crept into the thicket.

There *was* someone there. She could see them now, hunkered down and trying to hide from them. And it definitely was a someone, not a something, because it was blue — it was wearing clothes.

"I can see you there. Who are you?" asked Jani.

"You may as well come out," Penny added behind her.

There was a bit more rustling, then a sheepish, "Okay." A girl's voice. The figure clambered hesitantly through the bushes toward them.

Jani retreated from the thicket and waited, her hand on Keeta's neck. Even before the person stepped free of her cover, she recognized her. Kara. But what was she doing so deep inside the forest, hiding in a bunch of bushes? Was she hiding from *them*? But why?

The girl looked dirty and bedraggled when she stepped out from the undergrowth. Jani tried to look into her eyes, but Kara kept her gaze on the ground, stopping in front of Jani, Penny, and Keeta with hunched shoulders.

"Hey, have you seen some horses wandering around loose today?" Penny asked the question they'd been asking all day.

Kara gasped and looked up sharply. "Horses?" Her eyes darted left, then right. "You mean… normal horses?"

"Of course, normal horses," answered Penny. "What other kinds are there?"

Kara's gaze dropped back to the ground, her expression a strange mixture of relief and embarrassment. "I haven't, but if I do, what do they look like?"

"One's black, with a white spot on her chest," said Jani. "One's a palomino and the other is gray."

"What's palomino?"

"Gold body color, with a white mane and tail," Penny said. "He has four white socks too, and a blaze. A blaze is a white streak down his face."

Kara didn't say anything in response and the forest silence swelled thick around them. Jani glanced at Penny. Kara certainly was shy, almost to the point of seeming frightened of them. What did she think they were going to do to her? "If you see them, can you phone me or Penny?" she asked, her voice as kind as she could make it. No response. Maybe Kara didn't have a phone. "Or come to my house?" Jani added. "You know where I live?"

Kara nodded, whispered, "I think so."

"And if you see any other horses wandering about, let us know, okay?" added Penny. "There are eight missing altogether." She paused for a moment. "They might be together, hidden away somewhere too. It's possible they were stolen. Just tell us if you see *anything* suspicious."

A slight nod from Kara.

"We'd better be getting back," suggested Jani. "It's going to be dark soon." She felt like crying as the words came from her mouth. How could she stand going home, when all she wanted to do was search and search and search until she found her beloved Freedom?

57

She tightened Keeta's cinch again, and waited for Penny to climb up behind the saddle.

As Jani lifted her foot to the stirrup, she heard a soft, "wait," behind her. She lowered her foot and turned toward Kara.

"I…" The girl paused. Pushed at a stick with her foot, then looked tenuously at Jani. "I saw…" She stopped again.

"What?" asked Jani, hoping beyond hope. If only Kara had seen some sign of the horses. Any sign. It would be more than Jani and Penny had found. She wouldn't even care that Kara hadn't told them right away. As long as she told them now, that's what mattered.

Kara bit her lip, opened her mouth, closed it.

"What did you see?" Penny impatiently demanded from Keeta's back,

Jani poked Penny's knee without looking away from Kara. But it was too late. Kara's gaze dropped back to the ground, and Jani watched as her expression closed. "What did you see?" she asked, gently, just in case Kara would still tell her.

"Nothing. It was nothing. Just my imagination, that's all." Then Kara spun on her heel and ran into the forest.

That night, when Jani and Penny got back to Jani's house, they had a welcoming committee, and not a happy one. Both of Penny's parents were there, as well as her little brothers, and of course, Jani's parents. The crowd rushed out of the house when Jani and Penny rode Keeta into the driveway.

"Did you find them?" yelled Ben, Penny's oldest little brother.

"Find 'em? Find 'em?" Sammy screamed behind him, in his baby voice. Jani smiled, despite her misery. Sammy was still copying his big brother, his hero, in everything.

"No," Penny answered.

"Did you? Or the police?" Jani asked the adults.

Jani's mom shook her head tersely. "We were getting ready to come search for you. Do you know how late it is? How worried we've been? Anything could have happened to you out there!"

"Sorry," said Jani, tears catching at her voice. "I just couldn't stop, Mom. I kept thinking of Freedom out there all alone. Or in the hands of some horrible strangers. I just couldn't turn around."

"I understand, Jani. I just wish you had told us where you were going, then we could've found you when we started to worry." Her mom's voice wasn't much softer. She might understand, but she was still very upset.

"Or you should've waited until one of us got home," added her dad. "We would've gone with you."

"Come on, Penny," said Penny's mother. "It's past the boys' bedtime and you have school tomorrow."

"What? School? You can't expect me to go to school when Sunny's gone, Mom, Dad. You just can't!"

"We've already decided it would be for the best," said Penny's dad. "If the horses have been stolen, you'll be wasting your time searching. The authorities will catch them, and you girls don't need to miss school."

"You too, Jani," her mom said. Her voice was quiet, but firm.

"But what if they weren't stolen," Jani implore her dad. "What if they're hurt somewhere. Or lost." Of her two parents, he was always the easiest to persuade, and if she could influence him, he might be able to sway her mom and Penny's parents.

"We've made up a schedule between us to continue the search," said Jani's dad. "And you're not on duty until after school's out."

"Dad!"

"Sorry, Jani, but you can't miss school."

In the morning, both of her parents were just as adamant. After she took care of Keeta, she tried to convince them one last time, but they were ready for her arguments: they promised her they'd put posters up around town, ads on the radio and in the newspaper, and that they'd continue the search, one at a time so there was always someone around to guard Keeta, while she was in school. When Jani pointed out that she'd be a great help to them, they suggested that while she was at school, that she organize her friends into an after-school search party.

Finally, though she loathed to do it, Jani admitted defeat. She had no choice in this matter. It was that simple — and that incredibly hard! She always hated being told what to do, but this was a thousand times worse than any time before. One of her horses could be at risk! And her parents had no idea how important it was that *she* continue the search. The fact that Freedom was missing was her fault, and it should be *her*, not her parents, who saved the filly.

Penny met her at the front door of the school, a cross expression on her face. "You'll never guess what I found out this morning," she whispered to Jani.

"What?"

Penny looked over her shoulder. Mrs. Lindstrom and Mr. Carson, their Math and Science teachers, were walking down the sidewalk toward them, talking and laughing.

"Come on," said Penny, and she bolted across the lawn. Together they hurried away from the front doors, passed a couple of students lounging on the grass, and ducked around the corner of the building. Jani looked back around the corner. The teachers had gone inside. Neither must have thought anything suspicious about students obviously avoiding them.

"So what is it? Tell me," Jani asked. They didn't have to whisper now. They were far enough away from anyone who might hear.

"Kara's not at school."

"So?"

"So," Penny looked at her with exasperation. "I came early so I could ask her what she wanted to say to us yesterday. I mean, obviously she wanted to say something, but she chickened out. And anyway, she wasn't on her bus."

"So?" Jani's voice was puzzled.

"Don't you get it? She's avoiding us. So I got thinking, why would she want to avoid us? What secret is she keeping? And then I realized I've never, ever seen her parents."

Jani shook her head. "I don't get it. Why does that matter?"

Penny rolled her eyes. "Honestly, Jani, you'd make a terrible detective. You're so trusting. *Think*. Her reclusive parents? Horses missing? Kara acting nervous and suspicious?"

"But I…" Jani gasped. "So you're saying…"

"Yes! They could be the horse thieves!"

Jani leaned back against the school. "But Kara's been living here for a month, and the horses just barely went missing."

"But I was thinking, maybe that's how they make money. You know, move to a new town, stay a while so they're not suspected, then steal some of the best horses in town to sell somewhere, and finally move on to another place and do it all again. *And*," she added emphatically, "that would explain a *lot* of things about Kara too."

Jani frowned. Penny was right about that. It would totally explain why Kara didn't want to make friends — maybe her horse thief parents wouldn't let her. But still, there were other problems. "But she doesn't know anything about horses. Remember, she even asked you what a palomino was. Anyone who knows horses, knows that, right?"

A furrow appeared on Penny's forehead. She hadn't thought of that. "Maybe they've never stolen a palomino before." Then she brightened. "Or she was just trying to throw us off the trail."

"But I don't think she'd tell us anything if there was a chance her parents might get caught, and she did want to tell us *something* last night."

"Um, well… maybe she wanted to tell you because you've been so nice to her. Everyone else just ignores her, but you're always saying 'hi' to her." Penny sighed, then frowned. "Okay, so it doesn't make perfect sense. But you have to admit, it *might* be true."

"Yeah, it might," agreed Jani. "And it's the best lead we've had so far."

"The only lead we've had," Penny reminded her.

"Yeah. So let's go over to her house after school today," suggested Jani. "And you know, just snoop around. See if we can find anything suspicious."

"After we check with the parents to see if they found the horses." Penny looked at her sheepishly. "Just in case I'm jumping to conclusions. The first time ever, I might add."

Jani smiled. "Yeah, I can't remember *that* happening

63

before. Come on. The bell's going to ring and I can't be late." She grimaced. "Dad told me he's going to phone the school and check I'm here."

"Mine too! Where do parents learn these things? At some kid-torture school?"

This time Jani's feeble smile turned into a laugh. Penny could always do that to her. And it felt good to have a plan. At least that was something.

Kara wandered the forest like a wraith. That's how she felt anyway, like a ghost, insubstantial and unreal somehow. Like she was invisible, and no one saw her and no one cared. Like she was nothing but fog and air.

Ever since last Friday, the day she now thought of as Ketchup Day, her mom had changed completely toward her. She might have been growing more distant toward Kara for months — and angrier too — but at least she'd spoken to her. However, since Ketchup Day she hadn't said a single word to her daughter. It was true that Kara had been in the forest almost all day Saturday and Sunday, only coming home to sleep and eat some of the musty apples from the fridge, but on Sunday night she couldn't take the silence any longer. She listened to the TV from her room and ached to go downstairs, even though she was afraid her mom might shout or scream at her. But even that would be preferable to nothing.

Desperation made Kara descend the stairs. She walked into the living room, stood by the couch, and whispered, "Sandy," the name her mom insisted she use. Her mom looked at her once, so Kara knew she saw her, but she didn't make room for Kara to sit beside her, she didn't offer her any popcorn. She just ate, stared at the TV, and laughed along with the laugh track with a tight look on her face, as if there was a terrible smell in the room but she was too polite to say anything. Kara stood there for the longest five minutes of her life before she quietly backed out of the room.

This morning there had been no call to wake for school. No food except for the soggy apples. Kara headed out the back door hungry. There was only one place she could think to go, only one place she felt safe — the forest — and so she wandered among the giant trees like a shadow, not caring where she was or where she was going.

The music of running water touched her ears and she paused, looked around. Finally she spotted the tiny, flashing brook, tumbling down a mossy bank. She knelt beside it and dipped her hands into one of the pools. The water was a clear amber color like many coastal creeks, and icy cold. And she was so thirsty. She felt she'd been gone from home for hours already, though it felt like days too — weeks even.

It had been only three days since her mom pushed her out of her heart. How could one's life change so much in so little time? It seemed almost worse that she hadn't kicked Kara out. It was as if Kara wasn't even worth that stress, that effort, as if it was easier to simply forget her, knowing she would eventually go away on her own.

A sharp crack came from behind her and water drops went flying from Kara's hands as she spun around. Was it the unicorn?

This was no foal! And it wasn't a unicorn either! The black horse neighed in greeting, and stepped toward her,

her stride long and elastic. Kara stepped back and the coldness of the creek flowed around her ankles. She scrambled to the other side and turned again to face the strange horse. It had stopped and was looking at her, its ears pricked and its strange blue eyes bright with interest. It was then that Kara noticed the small white patch on the horse's chest.

"You're Jani's horse," she said, and her voice cracked with disuse. Except for Jani and Penny, she hadn't spoken to anyone for days. "What are you doing here? Don't you know they're looking for you?"

The horse lowered her head and whinnied in gentle response. Rather than jump the stream and take a chance she might startle the horse, Kara waded back through the water. When she came near, she held out her hand, and waited.

The horse didn't hesitate. It walked up to her like she was a long lost friend, nuzzled her hand, and pressed her head softly against Kara's heart. Cautiously, Kara reached to stroke the silky cheek.

"You're so beautiful," she whispered, and a rumbling nicker came from the horse. Kara leaned forward and inhaled deeply. The animal smelled so nice, like salty spice, and yet sweet too — a combination she'd never smelled before. "What's your name?" Jani and Penny had called out horses' names when they'd first heard her in the thicket. Sudden heat touched Kara's face. Even the thought of being caught hiding, and especially by Jani and Penny, made her feel embarrassed. She cleared her throat.

"Sunny?" she said, and watched the horse's reaction. Nothing. What was the other name she'd heard? "Freedom?"

The black filly lifted her head and whinnied softly. Kara smiled. She liked this horse. She seemed to be talking to her. "You're Freedom," she said, and the horse snorted.

"Come on, Freedom," said Kara. "I'll take you back to Jani's house. She'll be so glad to see you." She pulled gently on Freedom's forelock. The filly didn't budge. "Come on, girl," Kara said a little louder. Freedom merely raised her head, pulling her forelock from Kara's grasp. Then she took a step back.

"No, don't go!" Kara moved after Freedom to throw her arms around the horse's neck. It was the only thing she could think to do. But Freedom sidestepped her and turned, walked deeper into the forest.

"Freedom, please!"

The horse stopped. Looked back. Neighed.

Kara hurried after her, and Freedom stepped out again.

Kara stopped and so did Freedom. She neighed again. Took another step. Looked back. Neighed.

The girl inhaled deeply. "You want me to follow you."

Freedom whinnied again, and this time when she started to walk, Kara was right behind her. She followed the black horse through the trees for fifteen minutes before they got into territory unfamiliar to her.

"Wait, Freedom," she called out, and the black filly paused. Kara hurried to stand beside the horse. "Thanks," she whispered, and Freedom nickered and strode onward. Kara walked at her side, her hand on the soft mane.

The yearling walked steadily deeper into the wilderness, up and down hills, across gullies, through streams. Kara kept a sharp eye out for landmarks, the surrounding hills and unusual trees, as well as where the sun was positioned in the sky. She felt confident she could find her way back, as long as she was careful.

Suddenly they broke out of the forest and onto an old logging road. The road was overgrown, but still passable, even for a vehicle. And a vehicle had come this way recently. Kara could see the tracks.

"Let's go faster, Freedom," she encouraged. She had a sudden idea of where the horse was taking her, or more accurately, to whom. They made good time as they hiked along the twisting road, and then Kara noticed a spot of red ahead through the trees. At first she slowed, but when the horse kept striding onward, Kara ran after her — to round the corner and see a big red horse trailer sitting in a clearing, and beside it, a new corral.

"The gray," whispered Kara. "And there's the palo… palamano… uh, Sunny." And there were more horses too: three big brown ones, two of them with brown manes and tails, and one with a black mane and tail. And one fancy black and white spotted horse. But hadn't Penny said there were eight missing?

"They think you were stolen too, but you must've just broken out of your pen," she said to Freedom. She counted the horses in the corral again. Yes, there were only six. Seven, counting Freedom. So where was the eighth horse?

She saw movement along the back of the corral fence. A flash of white. Could it be? Her heart raced as the horse came into view around the outside of the corral. It was! The white unicorn foal!

Kara realized her mouth was hanging open and snapped it shut. Her hand clutched Freedom's mane as the foal moved closer. He stopped a few feet away from them, his head high and his ears pricked toward her. The black spot was clear on the top of his head. And she could see now she'd been wrong. It was just a spot — no horn would grow from the black hair. There was no horn bud, no bump.

One of the horses in the corral nickered and Kara looked up to see the spotted horse watching the foal carefully. His mother. He really was just an ordinary horse. There was nothing magical about him at all.

For a split second, she felt disappointment, then as quickly as it had arisen, the feeling vanished. There was something about this ordinary horse that made her feel all soft inside, as if he was magical anyway, at least to her. And wouldn't she be safer loving him more than loving a unicorn, some mythical creature that might run off to an alternate world at any moment?

Freedom nickered beside her, and Kara felt the dark horse nudge her forward. She reached out with a shaking hand. Would the beautiful foal allow her to approach him? Let her touch him?

A soft whinny like a whisper came from the foal, and she inhaled sharply at the sound. A small quake had shaken her core, like ripples in a pond, as if her soul had recognized his sound. As if she'd been waiting for him all of her life.

"Whisper," she murmured. "That should be your name. That's what I would name you, if you were mine." The foal sniffed at her hand, then stepped cautiously forward. Kara's fingers brushed against the baby hair on his neck. "So soft. Like a dove. I wish…" A long pause as she ran her hand along the top of his short silk mane. "If only…"

She bit her lip. There was no use even thinking the thought. Whisper would never be hers. Never. All she was doing with her feeble wishes was torturing herself. Whisper was one of the stolen horses. He had an owner, somewhere. An owner who would never sell him, just as she would never sell him if he belonged to her. And then there'd be her mom to convince too. It was nothing more than an impossible crazy dream.

But on second thought, was it really *that* impossible? Someone else had already stolen Whisper, and stealing from a thief wasn't really stealing, was it? And if she hadn't seen Jani and Penny yesterday, she wouldn't even know he'd been stolen. She might think he was a stray. Couldn't she just pretend she hadn't heard anything about stolen horses? And then as long as she kept him hidden away, he could be hers!

Freedom bumped her arm, and a nervous whinny filled the glade.

"What is it?" Kara stuttered. Had the black horse understood her thoughts? Instantly, she felt a flood of shame. What was she thinking? Of course it wouldn't be the right thing to do. And what if she got caught? Her mom would *never* forgive her for that.

Freedom nuzzled the foal, then whinnied loudly in the stillness. She bobbed her head up and down and backed toward the trees edging the clearing. The foal followed her. Shamefaced, Kara stood as if frozen. A distant rumble reached her ears, and with a gasp, she spun around. Someone was driving along the old road! She could hear their vehicle, even though it hadn't rounded the last corner yet. Freedom hadn't read her mind. She was trying to warn Kara of the returning thieves.

Kara ran into the forest after Freedom and Whisper. The black horse stopped in a thick cluster of bushes beneath the trees and touched the foal's back with her muzzle. She nickered softly. The foal whinnied back, then lowered himself to the ground.

Silently, Kara pulled a fallen bough closer to him and laid it between him and the corrals. If the thieves looked into the trees, they wouldn't see the dark horse in the thicket, but the foal was like a beacon drawing eyes to him. The better they could screen him the safer they would all be.

Just before the truck came into view, Kara hid behind a large fir tree. Cautiously she peeked around the edge of the rough bark. A big red truck entered the clearing and from what she could tell, there were two passengers inside. How close she had come to being caught!

The truck mowed over saplings and small bushes to

the corral, then the driver backed the vehicle in a tight turn. The passenger, a young man in denim jeans and a blue checked shirt, jumped out and guided the driver as he backed the truck toward the horse trailer.

A sharp whinny pierced the air. Whisper's mother! She was calling her foal!

With a racing heart, Kara hurried silently to the foal and crouched beside him. He had to stay where he was and remain silent, or the thieves might take him. Obviously, he'd slipped out of the corral, probably under the bottom rail because he was so small. The foal whisper-whinnied again, and automatically Kara reached out and touched his nose to quiet him. She looked toward the men. They hadn't heard him. The foal's soft neigh had been covered by the sound of the truck engine.

"Stop there!" The truck stopped in front of the trailer, and a second man got out of the cab. The two hitched the trailer to the truck.

"Okay, now let's do this as quick as we can. You catch them and I'll load them," the second man said. "It's a long way to Rambler, and we're behind schedule as it is."

Kara leaned to her right to peer through a space between bushes. She could see them now, untangling ropes and halters. The second man was wearing a brown shirt. Blue Shirt had his back to Kara, but she could see he had dark brown hair and wasn't as heavy as Brown Shirt. Brown Shirt looked like he was going bald on top too, so he must be the older of the two. She could see his face in profile and it looked as if wrinkles had made a permanent frown on his face.

Abruptly, Whisper whinnied again. Kara gasped and clamped her hand over his nose. Slowly, afraid of what she'd see, she looked through the bushes toward the two men. They'd heard him! They were standing completely still, looking toward the forest, and listening intently. Then the foal's mother let out a long call.

"I'll see what it is," the younger man said, and started jogging toward Kara, Freedom, and Whisper.

The bell rang. Jani snatched her pile of books from her desk and rushed out of the room. The day was taking forever. Freedom could be miles away by now and there were still two classes to go, Science and Gym — and she *hated* Gym. Especially today. How could her parents be so mean as to make her stay in school all day?

She reached her locker, spun the combination lock, opened the door, and threw her books on the top shelf. Now where, in all this mess, was her science book? She knelt and started riffling through the piles at the bottom of her locker.

"I've got to get out of here," Penny said beside her. Jani heard her friend's locker bang open and her books tumble inside. "I can't stand it anymore. It's torture to be in school when Sunny might be in trouble."

Jani closed her locker, and looked quickly up and down the hallway. No teachers in sight. "Hey, Penny, what do you think about skipping gym class? We could check all the trails behind the school, and then come back to catch the bus and finish organizing our search party. The parentals won't phone to check we're here for the *last* class of the day."

Penny's eyes lit up and she nodded her head. "Great idea. Now if we can just make it through Science…"

Kara crouched down beside the foal. The man was quickly coming nearer. What should she do? He was going to find them! And then what? What would they do to her? Should she run now, before he got too close? While she still had a chance to escape?

Something warm touched her back and she almost cried out before she realized it was Freedom. She looked up to see the black filly gazing at her with eyes of calm strength. Kara felt herself relax. Her breathing slow. No, she wouldn't run. She'd trust Freedom. The filly wasn't running. She was just standing, serene and peaceful, as if she knew...

"Don't worry about it," the older man called out, and Kara squeezed her eyes shut in relief. "Even if it's the foal, so what?" he continued. "We'll just leave him here. He won't last long after traveling all that way to find his dam."

"But what if he follows us out?"

Kara heard a loud snap. The younger man had just entered the forest and was breaking sticks as he walked. Only a few more yards and he'd see them! Why wasn't he turning around?

"He'd never make it," the older man said loudly.

"He's even farther from civilization now than when we first dumped him. And besides, we're in a hurry. You're wasting time."

"Okay, okay." The young man sounded reluctant and resentful, as if he hated taking orders. But still, he turned around.

Kara sagged silently to the forest floor. What would've happened if they'd found her and the horses? Would they have taken her captive? Added Freedom to the herd to sell? Killed Whisper? From what the older man said, they'd already tried to get rid of the foal by dumping him in the forest somewhere — probably somewhere near her house and that's why she'd seen him.

However, somehow, against all odds, the foal had found his way to his mother. And now the men were thinking they could leave him here, and that no one would ever find him. Well, they were already too late for that, thank goodness! *She* had found him — or rather, more accurately, she'd been led to him, and to the other horses as well.

Kara looked up at Freedom with renewed awe, and the filly's blue eyes burned into hers. Had Freedom found Whisper in the woods and taken him to his mother? Had she found him wandering the forest alone, just as she'd found Kara? But how could she know that a foal needed her, or where his mother was? Or that Kara needed someone to be kind to her, after all that had happened with her own mother? Kara shook her head. A horse couldn't know these things. And yet there was no other explanation.

"Okay, I'm ready for the last two," the older man said

and Kara looked through the bushes. He was walking down the trailer ramp. A clang came from inside the trailer and he spun around and yelled — to no avail. The thuds came regularly, loudly.

The young man haltered the last two horses within seconds. Obviously, he'd spent a lot of time around horses and knew how to handle them. The thuds were crashing in rhythm as the young man led the two prancing horses toward the trailer. "That mare's going to wreck our trailer," he said to the older man.

"She'll stop once we get moving." He reached to take one of the lead ropes from his assistant, but the horse snorted and sidestepped. The banging noise was making it nervous. The older man murmured to it, and the horse calmed, then he led the animal into the trailer. A few seconds later he was back for the last horse. When it was secured inside the trailer, the older man hurried down the ramp. "Let's get going. You got everything?"

"Sure do, Dad," the younger man said, sounding more cheerful now that the job was done. The tempo beating from inside the trailer increased as the two men closed the back door of the trailer.

Kara grimaced as the father and grown son moved swiftly toward the truck cab. So this horse stealing was a family business. The truck roared to life, and the trailer started to move. The father had been right. The mare did stop kicking as they slowly drove away, probably too off balance to do much with the trailer swaying and lurching over the rough road. Gradually the sound of the truck died in the distance.

Whisper whinnied and climbed to his hooves. This time Kara didn't stop him. He trotted through the trees to the corral, neighing searchingly as he went. He called again when he turned to look down the road, and this time his neigh was full of despair. Kara and Freedom stopped behind him.

"Sorry, little buddy," said Kara. She ran her hand along his soft back. "She's gone. I know you'll miss her, but try not to worry." His thick baby hair was almost wavy under her hand. "I'll take care of you. I promise."

She bent to hug the foal, then turned to Freedom. "And then I'll take you home, Freedom. We have to let Jani know about the stolen horses."

It was easier than Jani imagined to sneak away from the
school. She and Penny ducked out one of the back doors
on their way to the locker rooms, ran swiftly around the
edge of the sports field, and raced into the forest. They
crouched breathlessly behind a huge fir near the edge
of the field and peered out into the open. It seemed as if
they'd gotten away unseen. So far, so good.

"I think we need to split up if we want to check all the
trails back here," Jani said.

"Okay. You go right and I'll go left. We'll meet back
here in forty minutes." Penny glanced at her watch.

"Okay." Jani didn't hesitate. She broke into a swift
jog. They would have to hurry if they were going to
check all the trails near the school. The paths were a
maze, created by generations of school children, a maze
that Jani knew very well. She and Keeta had ridden here
countless times, both alone and with Penny and Sunny.

She inhaled deeply as she ran. The air in the forest
felt especially clear and vital after breathing the close air
inside the school all day. She could feel her body coming
alive, her mind sharpening, and then bending itself to
the problem: if Freedom wasn't stolen but had instead
opened her pasture gate, where would she go?

Immediately, Jani realized she was wasting her time searching the trails close to the school. They were well traveled by other kids too, and if someone had seen a horse wandering loose among the trees, she or Penny would've heard about it. She needed to check the trails farther away, the less traveled trails.

However, she'd only have time to check one or two sections of the distant trails before she had to turn back. She'd have to hurry. Jani ran faster, despite the sharp pain that was developing in her side. She wiped her brow with her sleeve. She hadn't slept well last night, having been tormented with thoughts of Freedom in trouble, and at one point she'd even gone down to the barn to check that Keeta was still safe in her stall. The lack of sleep, combined with hours of riding yesterday and massive amounts of worrying, were simply wearing her out. But she had to keep moving. She had to find the horses.

She was getting to the rougher trails now. The mountain that loomed behind the school was getting steadily nearer, the trail she was running, brushier. Jani slowed to a jog, then stopped when she came to a fork in the trail. Which way now?

She glanced at her watch. It was almost time to turn around. She'd been searching for 18 minutes. Two more minutes and she'd have to turn back to make her rendezvous with Penny and the school bus. But which way should she go? Her eyes scoured the ground.

And she saw hoof prints! Fresh hoof prints! Marking the trail from right to left. Jani sprinted down the left fork. After a few seconds, her breath was coming in gasps and her side felt it was being speared with a red hot lance. But still she kept running. Around another bend in the trail, and another.

And there she was! Freedom!

"Wait," Jani gasped. She tripped on a root and almost fell.

But Freedom heard her. The filly wheeled about and neighed loudly, then trotted back to Jani.

Jani flung her arms around Freedom's neck, madly blinking back a torrent of grateful tears. "I thought you were stolen, Freedom. I thought you were gone forever."

"I found her in the woods and was bringing her home to you." The voice came from behind Freedom on the narrow trail. "She led me to the stolen horses."

"Kara? You found them?" With an effort, Jani forced down her emotion. "The stolen horses?"

Kara nodded.

"Was Sunny with them?"

"Yeah. There were six of them in a corral." A strange expression flashed across the girl's face. "Only six," she repeated as if Jani was going to argue with her. "A gray one, Sunny, a black and white spotted one, and three brown ones. One of the brown ones had a black mane and tail."

A wonderful bubbling feeling rose up in Jani's chest. "Thank you, Kara! We owe you big time."

For a moment, the serious look lingered on Kara's face, and then her expression relaxed into a small, cautious smile. "Thanks," she said and reached to stroke the filly's sleek side. "But it was mainly Freedom."

"Now you just need to show us where they are," said Jani.

The strange expression reappeared. "They're gone. The thieves took them in a trailer."

Jani felt the blood drain from her face. "Poor Sunny. Where? Do you know?"

"They said something about Rambler. That's a town, right?"

"Yes! And I bet I know why they're going there too. Rambler has a big horse sale every spring. They must be taking them there to sell!"

"You found her!"

Jani grinned as she hurried toward Penny, Freedom and Kara close behind. "Kara found her. Or rather, Freedom found Kara."

"And the others?"

"Them too."

Penny clasped her hands in front of her and rolled her eyes heavenward. "Thank you, thank you, thank you," she whispered.

"They *were* stolen. And it's not over yet, Penny. Kara saw the thieves load them into a trailer."

Penny's face blanched.

"But don't worry," Jani added quickly. "They're taking them to Rambler. Probably to the horse sale. We have to find out when it starts."

"What if it started already? What if they've sold him and he's gone forever?" Penny said, her voice shrill. Her hands twisted around each other in her anxiety.

"Don't worry. We'll get him back," Kara said quietly. She put a gentle hand on Penny's shoulder.

"That's right," Jani said firmly. "But we need to act fast. First, let's take Freedom home through the back trails. And as soon as we get to my house, we'll phone

Officer Hughes and tell him the horses were taken to Rambler." She reached to grab the black's mane. "Come on, Freedom."

"What?" Even though Kara's voice was quiet, it reverberated with panic. "You can't call the police."

Both Jani and Penny looked at her curiously. "Why not?" asked Penny.

"Nothing, I just… I mean…" Kara scuffed the ground with her foot.

"But we have to phone. The police need to arrest the thieves," Jani explained.

"Officer Hughes is really nice," offered Penny. "We've already talked to him and he's not bossy or anything. There's nothing to worry about. Really."

Kara paused for a long moment, and Jani could see the struggle on her face — both fear and the desire to trust. Finally, Kara's gaze skipped from Penny to Jani to Freedom. "Okay," she whispered.

When they broke out of the trees and onto the side lawn at Jani's house, Freedom neighed loudly and cantered toward the pasture fence. Keeta answered her and leapt into a gallop. The two met at the fence, snuffling and nickering softly to each other.

"Jani! You found her!" Jani's mom leaned over the railing on the back porch. "Where was she? What about the others?"

Jani ran toward the house. "You have to phone the police right away, Mom. Kara saw the stolen horses and heard the thieves talking."

"Is that Kara?" Jani's mom asked, peering off toward the trees.

Jani spun around to see only Penny behind her.

Penny rolled her eyes. "I'll go get her. Kara's a little shy," she explained.

Jani's mom nodded. "I'll go make that call, and I'll phone your dad too, Jani. He's been out searching all afternoon."

Jani's dad arrived shortly before Officer Hughes. At first, Kara hardly spoke to the Officer, leaving it up to Jani to tell about the horses. When Jani told him of the comment Kara overheard about Rambler and the fact that there was a big horse sale there every spring. Jani's dad jumped up and went to the phone.

"Smart thinking," he said when he returned. "The sale starts tomorrow at 8 a.m."

Officer Hughes made a note of this, then turned to Kara. "Now Kara," he said kindly. "Can you give me descriptions of the men and the horses you saw?"

In a small voice, Kara told him the color of the men's hair, their approximate ages, and what they were wearing. Then she gave him a detailed description of each of the horses, which he checked against a list. She seemed to remember the horses a lot better than the men, but Jani understood. She always noticed horses before people too. Then Officer Hughes asked Kara if she could take him to the corral where the thieves had kept the herd.

Kara's eyes darted toward the door, as if more than anything she wanted to escape. "N…no. I don't think I can find it again," she said, hunching her shoulders. "I didn't follow a trail or anything. I just followed Freedom."

"Freedom?"

"She's my horse, the one we called about yesterday," explained Jani. "But she wasn't stolen. I guess Penny and I *didn't* latch the gate right. Anyway, she led Kara to the stolen horses."

"You mean…" The Officer paused. "You mean your horse found the stolen horses, and then went looking for someone to show them to?" He sounded incredulous.

"She's smart," was all Jani could think to say.

"She must be. And she found Kara in the forest too

89

— during school hours." He paused and Kara fidgeted uncomfortably on the couch. "This one time, skipping school turned out to be a good thing," the Officer continued. "But you need to take better care of your future, Kara. You need to go to school, just like everyone else." His voice was firm.

"One thing Kara said," interjected Penny, "was that there were only six horses in the corral. You said on the phone that, counting Freedom, there are eight missing. So where's the seventh horse? Did they sell it already?"

Officer Hughes sighed and put down his notebook. "I hate to say it, but there's only one explanation for the seventh horse. The thieves probably…" He paused for a moment, as if he was thinking which words to choose. "…uh, got rid of him."

"What do you mean?" asked Jani. She felt sick.

"He's a Medicine Hat Paint foal," the Officer continued. "Very rare, and therefore very recognizable. They'd be foolhardy to try to sell him. Even selling a mare and foal, when there are a pair missing, might be risky for them."

"A Medicine Hat Paint?" asked Jani's dad. "Sorry, but what's that?"

"A white horse with a black 'hat,' or spot, between or over its ears and forehead. The Native Americans considered them sacred horses with powers to protect their riders." He looked at Kara, and added hopefully, "You didn't see any sign of a foal in the forest, did you?"

Kara swallowed. "No," she croaked.

"That's a shame," said Officer Hughes. "Well, that's

it then." He snapped his notebook shut and rose to his feet. "I'll call the police in Rambler and forward the descriptions to them. I'm sure they'll check out the sale barns as soon as they can."

Penny jumped up. "You'll tell us as soon as you hear anything, right?"

Officer Hughes smiled. "Of course." He turned to Kara, huddled on the corner of the couch. "You won't be skipping school again, will you, Kara? You wouldn't want your parents to be disappointed in you."

The girl looked at him with wide haunted eyes. "You won't tell my mom, will you?" Her voice trembled.

A frown touched Officer Hughes' face. He shook his head. "No, not this time." He said the words slowly, thoughtfully.

"I gotta go." Kara sprang off the couch and hurried to the front door. Jani quickly followed her. At the door, Kara paused. "Bye, Jani."

"Thanks for bringing Freedom home."

Kara looked down at the floor. "She's a nice horse."

"She likes you too, I can tell." When Kara looked up at her with a spark of interest in her eyes, Jani continued. "You can come visit her, and me, any time you want, you know."

"Thanks," whispered Kara. She sounded like she was going to cry. Then she was gone, the door closing softly behind her.

Kara hurried along the road toward home, moving at a quick jog. What a wonderful, terrible day it had been: being found by Freedom, seeing Whisper again, and then being interrogated by the police officer! Not that he'd been mean, but she'd come so close to telling him the truth about the foal. It had taken all her courage to lie to him, plus every bit of strength and willpower she had.

And she'd almost had a heart attack when she thought he might tell her mom about her skipping school! How beyond horrible that would've been. Her mom would flip out if he even set foot on their property. She'd probably pack up everything they owned and force Kara to leave with her that night — and what would happen to Whisper then, alone in the thieves' corral, more than a mile inside the forest? He would be truly abandoned then. No one knew where he was, or even that he was alive, other than her.

However, she'd been lucky. The policeman *was* a nice guy and said he wouldn't tell her mom. And he hadn't asked to drive her home either. He hadn't done anything but look at her strangely a time or two, and she was used to that.

Now she needed to find something to feed the foal.

He would be getting hungry. She'd heard on the TV that horses like apples, and thankfully, there were still some apples left at home.

She slowed to a walk when she reached the long driveway that led to the house she and her mom rented. If her mom had finished ignoring her, then she'd need a plan to get away. It was important that she get food and water to Whisper soon, so she had to find a bucket, fill it with apples, and slip into the forest without being seen. The house came into sight around a bend in the driveway and Kara paused. If her mom wasn't in front of the TV…

Suddenly, she stiffened. What was that sound? A car was coming slowly down their driveway behind her! Had her mom gone somewhere?

But, no. Her mom's beat up, old car was in front of the house.

Kara ran to the side of the driveway and dove into the forest. She hunkered down behind a bush, and peered through the leaves — and what she saw made her wince. A police car came slowly around the bend and crept past her over the rough road, Officer Hughes at the wheel. He'd changed his mind! He was going to tell her mom she'd been ditching school.

Kara buried her head in her hands. What should she do now? Try to stop him from driving the rest of the way to the house? But she was already too late. He was within view of anyone looking out a window. And her mom would be looking. She would have heard the car by now. As she watched, the police officer parked beside her mother's car in front of the house.

Wild thoughts streamed through Kara's head, ideas that she knew wouldn't work even as she thought them. It was too late. The damage had been done. An hour after the Officer left, they would be in the car, driving on to a new town, a new life. A life without Whisper.

Officer Hughes knocked on the door. And waited. Knocked again. Then called out a greeting. There was no response, so he walked around the side of the house toward the backyard.

Kara said a silent prayer that her mom wasn't trying to go out the back door. She was just that way, always thinking everyone was out to get her. She might even try to hide in the forest until the police officer was gone.

Just like I'm doing, thought Kara. *But I have no choice. I have Whisper to think of.*

And suddenly, Kara knew there was one way, and one way only, that she could be sure Whisper wouldn't be left alone to die in the corral. There was one way that she wouldn't be torn away from him, if not today, then certainly another day. And there was more to it too: she was tired of moving on. She wanted to stay here where she had a beautiful foal for a friend, and maybe two more friends if she counted Freedom and Jani. Or three, if Penny became less irritated with her. There was only one way she could stay in Red River. She had to run away from home.

Jani turned off the TV with a frustrated jab at the remote control. "I hate this waiting. Why don't they call?" she complained.

Penny rolled over on the rug in front of the TV and grimaced. "I know. Maybe we should call them."

"Mom says I can't." Jani kicked the coffee table.

Penny started to thump her feet against the floor. "Ring. Ring. Ring," she chanted to the phone between each thump. It didn't ring.

"I know!" Jani leapt toward the phone. "Just wait!" She stabbed some numbers into the keypad. "Dad… No, we haven't heard anything… I had an idea… Of course it's a good idea. I wouldn't call you if it wasn't." She rolled her eyes at Penny, and covered the receiver for a moment. "Parentals," she whispered, then spoke into the receiver again. "I just thought, why don't *we* go to the sale? No one will be able to identify Sunny like Penny, and Kara's the only one who's seen the thieves. We'll ask her to come too… Great! Call us right back!"

Her eyes shone as she set the receiver down. "He's going to phone Officer Hughes and make sure it's okay."

Penny sat up. "That would be so awesome! I'd *love* to help catch the guys who stole my Sunny."

The phone rang and Jani jerked up the receiver. "What'd he say?... Sorry. Hello, Father Dear, how are you? Now tell me, please!" A breathless pause. "Yes! Thanks, Dad! We'll go over and talk to Kara right now... No, she doesn't have a phone... Yes, I know where she lives. She told Officer Hughes, remember?" As Jani recited the address, Penny hurried to pull on her shoes. Within seconds, the two girls were out the door.

"You want to take Keeta?" asked Penny.

"No, she needs a rest." They hurried down the driveway. "You know, I never thought of it before, but it is kind of weird that Kara doesn't have a phone."

Penny shrugged. "Some people don't like technology."

"I guess," said Jani. "I'm just glad she lives nearby. I'd hate to have to hike across town."

When they arrived at Kara's driveway, they slowed down. The driveway was pitted and potholed, and when the house came into sight, it was rundown and neglected. The lawn hadn't been mowed all spring, and the sunlight reflecting on the dirty windows made it impossible to see inside.

"Creepy," Penny whispered as they climbed the rickety stairs to the front door.

"Yeah," Jani agreed. "I'd hate to live here." She knocked timidly on the door. The sound echoed through the small house. "Do you hear anything?" she asked Penny, and leaned closer to the door. A faint thud.

"An inside door closing? Maybe she's coming."

They waited another minute. Jani knocked again, and when the silence stretched on, she added, "It could've been the back door. Maybe she didn't hear us because she's out back doing something."

"Let's go see."

The two girls walked through the shin-high grass and around the side of the house. Cautiously, they peered around the corner. The backyard seemed deserted. Jani sighed. "But someone *was* here. We heard them."

"Maybe it was a cat or something," suggested Penny.

"So what do we do now? We really need Kara to come." Jani kicked a soda can lying in the grass and it went spinning toward a ramshackle shed.

"Maybe if we just hang around a bit, she'll…"

The shed door crashed open. A woman burst out and marched toward them with a furious expression on her face! "You get out of here! She's mine! I won't let you have her!"

Penny shrieked and ran, and Jani found herself backing up, very quickly. "We just want to talk to Kara," she managed to say.

"You corrupted her! You sent the police!" Kara's mom was screaming now, her furious eyes locked on Jani as she strode toward her.

"I didn't. We didn't. What are you talking about?"

The woman was gaining on her, her face twisted into a hideous mask. "She's mine! You can't have her! She's mine!"

She was so close now that Jani could see her white knuckles.

"Jani, run!" Penny yelled behind her. "She's not going to stop!"

Jani ran. The woman was crazy. There was no point in trying to reason with her. They were around the side of the house and racing across the overgrown lawn within seconds. Halfway down the rutted driveway, Jani stopped, her expression wild with panic. There was no one in sight. The house looked as lonely as it had when they arrived.

"Come on, let's get out of here," said Penny insistently. "She might be sneaking through the woods or something. She's totally insane."

Jani nodded. "Poor Kara," she said, her voice still trembling from the bizarre encounter. "If that's her mom, no wonder she's scared of everybody." Together they jogged the rest of the way down the driveway and turned onto the road. Within a few minutes, they were back at Jani's house. They briefly checked the answering machine, but there were no messages saying the horses had been found.

"Do you think Kara's okay?" Jani asked, her hand lingering on the phone. "I mean, maybe we should tell someone that her mom is totally nuts."

"She might get mad," said Penny. "If she wanted people to know, she'd tell them, right?"

"Maybe." Jani shivered. "Let's go brush the horses. That always helps me think."

Freedom was standing at the gate when they walked out the back door. When she saw Jani and Penny, she neighed loudly, bobbed her head, and struck the ground with her front hoof.

Jani stopped short. "Hey Penny, you're going to think

I'm crazy too, but that's exactly what Freedom was doing when she tried telling me about the stolen horses."

"Yeah, I remember, when we rode off on Keeta to look for Sunny."

"And then she got out herself and found Kara in the woods."

"So you think… what?" Penny looked at her. "That she'll find Kara for us now?"

"I don't know, but she obviously wants out for a reason. And this time, I'm not going to make her break out to do whatever it is she wants to do."

Penny grinned. "Another game of 'Follow the Filly.' There's never a dull moment with Freedom around."

Freedom led them straight as an arrow through the forest. She tramped between bushes, around trees, and through creeks, completely ignoring any trails. Behind her, Keeta carried Jani and Penny at a brisk walk.

"She certainly has a destination in mind," Penny said in wonderment, and ducked just in time to avoid some low branches.

"I'm just glad I listened to her this time. I felt so guilty after she disappeared."

"Any idea of what she wants to show us?"

Jani shook her head, and in front of them, Freedom stopped to look back. She whinnied softly, then continued on much slower, her step quieter. Keeta too began to walk more cautiously, taking care not to step on any twigs. "Whatever it is, she wants us to see it before it knows we're here," whispered Jani.

She could see an opening in the forest canopy ahead now. Freedom stopped and Keeta stopped beside her. The girls slid quietly from the mare's back and crept forward.

"Oh my." Jani couldn't stop the soft exclamation.

"Oh my, is right. She lied to us and to Officer Hughes."

Jani breathed deeply. "She decided to keep the foal for herself."

Kara was incredibly relieved to see Whisper still inside the corral when she arrived. He was so small that she'd been afraid he'd slip beneath the bottom rail and go looking for his mother. However, the beautiful white foal was waiting for her with his whispery whinny and his tiny ears perked forward.

Her relief was short-lived. Whisper was obviously hungry and thirsty. He kept nuzzling her and nickering, but she didn't have anything to feed him. She hadn't gotten the apples or bucket because the policeman had arrived, and she had no rope to lead the foal to the nearby creek. She scoured the ground around the corral thinking maybe the thieves had left something she could carry water in, but their lawbreaking didn't seem to include littering.

"Will you follow me to the creek and then back here, little Whisper?" she asked the foal softly. He nuzzled her again, whinnied. "I guess we have to try. But please, *please,* don't run away, okay? Your mom isn't anywhere near here."

"Kara!"

Kara spun around. Who was there?

Jani and Penny. What a relief! They wouldn't tell. They knew what it was like to love a horse.

102

The two girls, Freedom, and Keeta advanced on the corral.

"You lied to us," said Penny. "You lied to the police."

"I had to," Kara said defiantly, then stepped back, surprised at the vehemence in her own voice. But what she said was true. She *had* to keep Whisper. She belonged with him. She knew that more than she knew anything.

The two girls stopped at the fence and looked at each other. Kara could read their unspoken communication as easily as if it had been aloud. They weren't going to keep her secret. Tears brimmed in her eyes and spilled down her cheeks.

"You can't keep him here," Jani said with compassion, as if she knew exactly what Kara was feeling. "Come to the fence. I want to show you something."

Reluctantly, Kara moved to stand beside the two girls. Whisper stayed where she left him, his head hanging low.

"Do you see how thin he is?" asked Jani. "You can count all his ribs. And his legs are trembling, see?" When Kara nodded, she continued. "He needs mare's milk, or a substitute, to survive. He's not old enough to leave his dam."

"But, I can't…" Kara whispered.

"Yes, you can," Penny said firmly. "If you really love him, you *can* give him up. It's the only way to save him."

Tears dripped off Kara's chin. "I do love him," she gasped. The foal, hearing the distress in her voice, walked toward her on shaky legs.

"We can bring him back to my house," said Jani.

"Mom will pick up some milk substitute for him at the feed store."

"And you won't tell the police, or his owners?" Kara raised her head in sudden, unrealistic optimism. Would Jani and her parents let her keep Whisper at their house?

"We have to," explained Penny. "He belongs with his dam, and by tomorrow she should be back home."

The beautiful white foal wandered the last few steps and stopped beside them. Gently, Kara hugged him. He felt so fragile in her arms. So delicate. How she loved him! And yet even though she knew her heart would break, she would give him up.

It took them a couple of hours to encourage the weakened foal back to Jani's house. They let him stop to rest whenever he wanted, and sometimes it took Freedom nudging him, or the girls leading Keeta and Freedom onward, to get the foal to move again. At the first creek they came to, Whisper drank, his thin white muzzle barely breaking the water's surface. He revived after that for a little while, but by the time they were among the giant trees near Jani's home, he was hardly moving.

"Let's stop for a minute," Penny said.

Jani stopped the horses and turned back to Penny and Kara. One girl was standing on each side of the foal. "But we're almost there."

The foal sunk to his trembling knees, then groaned and lay on his side. Maybe a rest was a good idea.

"Hey, Kara," Jani said, walking back to the two girls, "I forgot. We need to ask you a favor — to come with us to the sale and help identify the thieves."

"Uh, yeah," added Penny. "And we went to your house today to ask you."

Kara's face went white. "You went to my house?"

Jani exchanged a glance with Penny. "Yeah. We met your mom." Kara inhaled sharply and shut her eyes. "She was kind of…" Jani searched for the right word, but there weren't any nice ones. "Scary," she concluded, quietly.

"What do you mean?"

Freedom nickered and moved around the outside of their little circle to stand over Kara.

"Don't be mad, okay?" said Penny.

"Just tell me." Kara sounded defeated, not angry.

"Kind of crazy scary," explained Penny. "She yelled that we were trying to steal you away. Things like that."

Kara's eyes were large and dark in her thin face. "You think she might be crazy?" Her voice was the faintest whisper.

"We don't *want* to think she's crazy," said Jani. "And maybe she isn't. She just acted that way. Sorry."

Kara stroked Whisper's neck. "Don't say you're sorry. It's not your fault. And she didn't use to be that way. Just the last couple of years she's been changing." She paused to sniffle. "I thought it was *my* fault, because I was doing everything wrong."

"It's your fault that she's… uh, nuts?"

Kara nodded. "I always say or do something to bother her. Sometimes I just bug her by breathing, and she gets so mad. Yells at me. And lately it's been getting worse." She paused and covered her face with her hands. "I… I thought I was poison to her. To everyone. And then… then…" Her small sob seemed loud in the forest stillness.

Jani touched Kara's shoulder. "You can trust us. We won't tell anyone, if you don't want us to."

Kara pushed tears from her cheeks. "And then last Friday, she got mad at me again, and said she couldn't stand the sight of me. She says I'm becoming more and more like this person called Marjorie, that she *hates*." Kara sounded like she was forcing the words past gritted teeth. "I thought I was going to die I hurt so bad, but then Whisper appeared in a ray of sunshine. He made me feel…." Jani and Penny waited as Kara collected her emotions. "He made me feel special. And then Freedom found me, and she liked me too." The black filly nuzzled Kara's hair and nickered, and the girl sniffled as she reached up to stroke the satin face. She smiled sadly through her tears. "And I started to wonder. For the very first time I wondered if… maybe… I *am* likeable. And if my mom is just sick."

"You should tell someone about this — an adult, I mean," said Penny.

"No. You said…"

"And we won't. We promised. We won't say a word," Jani said quickly. "Not unless you want us to. But be careful, okay, Kara? Your mom really scared us."

"And she could have hurt us too," said Penny. "She acted like she wanted to. What if she hurts you?"

"I'll be okay. Lately she's been treating me like I don't exist."

"So you're safe as long as she ignores you?"

"I can't turn her in. She *is* my mom."

Jani sighed. "I don't know what I'd do either, if it was me."

"Me either," admitted Penny.

Kara's fingers slid through the short white mane. "What about Whisper? You guys won't tell anyone I was planning on keeping him, will you?"

"Course not," said Penny, rising to her feet. "We'll say we all found him in the forest."

Freedom nudged Whisper with her nose, and the foal climbed shakily to his hooves.

"So can you come to the sale with us, Kara?" asked Jani, and then added reluctantly, "Do you want us to go with you when you ask your mom? My dad can take us over. She might not freak out at us then."

"No. I mean yes, I want to come with you, but I don't want to ask. I'm *not* going to ask. I'll just come."

"She won't worry?"

Kara laughed, but the sound wasn't cheerful. "Unless someone else shows up at the house that she can yell at, she won't even notice I'm gone."

Dusk was well advanced by the time they finally got to Jani's house. As they helped the foal across the back lawn, Jani called out to the house. When there was no response, Freedom stopped, put her head high in the air, and neighed loudly. The back door opened moments later and Jani's parents rushed out.

"Where have you girls been?" Her mom's words tumbled over one another.

"I went to the address you gave me," Jani's dad said, sounding almost sick. "No one was there. The house seemed deserted. I had no idea what happened to you."

Jani looked at Kara in the half light. When Kara slightly shook her head, Jani said, "I'm really sorry, Dad. We were only there a couple of minutes." She looked down at the ground. How she hated misleading him! But she'd promised Kara she wouldn't say anything. "We went looking for the thieves' corral, and then look what we found on our way home." She motioned to the foal, as if her parents hadn't already seen him between them. "We need to phone the vet. He's very weak."

Jani's dad seemed relieved to have a distraction from his worries. "I'll do that right away. Then I'll then call

Penny's parents and Officer Hughes, too. He'll be glad about the foal."

"Have they found the horses yet?" Penny asked before he could leave.

"Not yet. Officer Hughes said something else came up and he's been busy. The police in Rambler checked the sale yard but the stolen horses weren't there yet. Be right back." He spun around and hurried into the house.

"He thinks they'll probably take the horses to the sale in the morning, rather than risk keeping them there overnight," Jani's mom added. "So don't worry. Sunny will be fine."

Penny smiled gratefully at Jani's mom.

"You'll have to leave by midnight, if you want to make it there before the sale starts," she added.

"You're not coming, Mom?"

She shook her head. "I'll stay and take care of the horses tomorrow, and I'll care for them tonight too. You girls need some rest before you leave. You've been running all over the country the last few days."

"I am tired," Jani admitted.

"There's some chili on the stove, so be sure to eat before you go to bed. Penny, you can use the cot, as usual, and Kara, you can sleep on the couch. I'll take care of the foal until the vet arrives." Her hand lingered across the baby's neck.

"But…" Kara's word was soft, as if she was afraid to speak. She bit her lip.

"But Kara wants to stay with Whisper," Jani said, guessing what her new friend wanted to say.

110

Jani's mom smiled at Kara. "But of course she does. How silly of me. Let's lead the horses out to the barn, Kara. You can help me take care of Freedom and Keeta too. I've been practicing my grooming skills, so I can show you how to do it, if you want."

A tentative smile touched Kara's face. "That sounds fun."

As the two of them led the horses away, Penny leaned toward Jani. "Just what Kara needs. A grown up that doesn't yell at her. Maybe she'll get braver. But there *is* a danger, you know."

"What's that?" Jani yawned.

"She's going to fall in love with both your horse *and* your mom."

She was riding Freedom, leaning over the ebony neck, her hands wrapped in the thick mane. The horse skimmed over the ground like a raven, dark and sleek, her hooves barely touching the ground.

"Jani?"

Freedom snorted in mid-stride and leapt into the air in an effort to avoid the voice. She was flying now, higher and higher. The golden plain fell beneath her and the purple mountains shortened beside her.

"Jani, wake up."

And then the black was floating back to earth, dissipating beneath her like a cloud. Gone.

"Freedom," croaked Jani.

"Jani!" A hand touched her shoulder. "It's time to wake up. The sale, remember?" Her mom's voice.

Jani opened her eyes. Stretched. Yawned.

"You can sleep on the way to Rambler. But now you need to get up and dressed."

Jani sat up and glanced sleepily in Penny's direction. Her friend was sitting on the edge of the cot, her eyes half open and her hair sticking out. She looked like she might tip over sideways. "You look like a bear that's just woken up after a long winter," Jani teased.

Penny grabbed her pillow and threw it weakly at Jani. It bounced off the floor in front of her and hit her ankles.

"You're about as strong as one too," added Jani.

"Are you both awake now?" asked Jani's mom from the doorway. "You won't go back to sleep the minute I leave, will you?"

"No, we're up," said Penny, rising to her feet. She walked groggily toward the bathroom. As she passed Jani's bed, she scooped up the pillow, whacked Jani across the head, and ran.

"I'll get you!" Jani yelled and sprinted toward bathroom door, only to have Penny slam it in her face and lock it.

"Obviously you're both well awake. I'll go make some sandwiches for your trip. And Jani, you can go wake Kara."

"Where is she?" Jani was already slipping on her jeans.

A soft look came over her mom's face. "She's still in the barn. She wanted to spend as much time with Whisper as she could. By the time she gets back, he might be gone."

Jani pulled on some clean socks. "She sure does like him, and he likes her too. It's sad."

"It is," agreed her mom.

The light was on in the barn when Jani opened the door. Both Freedom and Keeta looked at her as she entered, then both closed their eyes again to sleep.

"Kara? Are you here?" Jani moved to the first extra stall. It was empty. Had Kara weakened in her resolve to save Whisper and stolen the foal away? But no, there they were, in the second extra stall. The foal lay on his side, and Kara was curled up against his back, her arm over his shoulders. Jani could see dried tear tracks on her face. Quietly, she opened the door, but not quietly enough. The foal raised his head.

"Hello, little Whisper. You're looking much better. Was that milk substitute good?"

Abruptly, Kara sat up and took in her surroundings with a wild gaze. Frightened eyes stopped on Jani. "Stay away!"

Even before she said anything, Jani could see remembrance dawn on Kara's face. "It's time to leave for the sale," she said.

"I was dreaming," said Kara, as she looked at the foal. "I was riding Whisper and he was grown up, and I was so happy. But there was a shadow following us." She looked up at Jani and Jani saw new tears in her eyes. "I'm going to miss him so much, Jani. This might be the last time I ever see him."

"No, it won't," said Jani, unable to stand the misery in Kara's eyes. "Mom and Dad will take us to visit him. I'm sure they will, as long as you're allowed."

Kara's gaze fell. "As long as I'm allowed." She sighed, and her fingers slid through the white silk mane. She bent to kiss the foal on his black spot. "I love you, Whisper," she murmured. "And I'll never forget you. Ever. As long as I live. You'll always be my magical unicorn."

Then she was on her feet and rushing out of the stall, out of the barn, leaving behind a confused Jani, a sleepy Keeta, a sorrowful Freedom, and a tiny foal named Whisper to whinny after her, unheard.

The drive to Rambler took longer than they thought it would. They hadn't factored in the extra time it would take to pull a horse trailer, or that they might come across road construction. When they reached the second flag person holding a stop sign, Penny groaned aloud. "We're never going to get there in time. Never."

"We'll only be a few minutes late, Penny," said Jani's dad, trying to console her. "And the police should be there already, looking for the horses and thieves. There's nothing to worry about."

The minutes stretched past. The flag person held the stop sign like a statue.

"She's never going to let us go," Penny's voice was almost a wail. "And they're selling him right now. I can feel it. He'll be gone by the time we get there."

Just then, the flag person flipped her sign to the side that read "SLOW".

"Go! Go!" yelled Penny.

"Enough of that," Jani's dad said, looking at Penny sternly through the rear view mirror. "It won't help Sunny to yell or panic. We won't get there any faster."

"Sorry, Mr. Preston," said Penny sheepishly. "But please, *please, PLEASE* hurry."

Penny was almost hyperventilating by the time the big sale barn, with its surrounding corrals and stable rows, came into view. "There it is!" she shrieked, and Mr. Preston jumped. Jani and Kara both covered their ears.

"Sorry," Penny said again.

They had to park some distance from the arena, as the sale had started and all the nearby parking places were taken. As they hurried down the long driveway to the sale barn, Jani's gaze jumped from horse to horse in the corrals they passed, lingering on any palomino, pinto, or gray horses.

There, a palomino! Her heart thudded madly and she opened her mouth to say something, but stopped. Penny was hurrying past the horse, and Jani could see now that it wasn't Sunny. It was a young horse, a two- or three-year-old. Penny hadn't been fooled for a moment.

"Do you see any of the stolen horses, Kara?" asked Jani's dad.

Kara shook her head, her eyes slightly alarmed. "There are so many brown ones, and I can't tell them apart."

"What about the others?" asked Jani.

"That one looks kind of like Sunny, but it doesn't have white legs." She pointed at the palomino Jani had noticed. "I don't see the gray horse or the spotted one either."

"What about the thieves?"

Kara shook her head. "No. Sorry. I'm no help at all."

"There are lots of stalls and corrals behind the main sale barn too. They might be there," suggested Jani, then added, "Don't worry, Kara. You'll recognize them when you see them."

"We need to find Officer Hughes," said Jani's dad. "While I look for him, you girls can search these front corrals for the horses."

"Sure," said Jani.

"And if you see them, come find me immediately. *Don't* approach them, even if the horses seem to be alone. Even if you see Sunny. We don't want the thieves to get suspicious before the police arrive." He paused for a moment, and in the silence, a horse neighed loudly. "So, *promise* me you'll come find me, okay?"

"We will," Jani and Kara said together.

"Penny?" he asked, suspicious of her silence. "I need a promise from you too."

The girl's face was turned away and she was staring at a horse on the other side of the corrals, near the side of the complex. A buckskin. A man was trying to load the horse into his trailer, but it was refusing to cooperate. The horse kept pulling back and Jani could see the buckskin's new owner was getting angry. He snapped the lead rope and the horse reared, then neighed again, loudly.

"Sunny! It's Sunny," gasped Penny, spinning around to face them. "They colored his mane and tail and legs, but it's him. I know it is!" And then she was running pell-mell toward the balking horse.

"Go find Officer Hughes," Jani's dad commanded, and raced after Penny.

Jani and Kara dove into the crowd that surrounded the sale barn. How were they going to find the officer in this mass of people? The Officer said he'd be here, but where? Inside the sale barn? Out by the corrals? Back by the stables? They had to find him quick! They'd only seen one man with Sunny, but that didn't mean the second thief wasn't there too, lurking just out of sight — and if the thief called his partner for help, Jani's dad would be facing *two* men. What would they do to him?

Kara grabbed Jani's arm. "Is there anywhere we can get higher, so we can look down on the crowd?"

"Yes! The bleachers, inside the sale barn. This way!" Jani ducked under a woman's arm, around a big man's stomach, and was through the double doors. She hurried toward the bleachers, dodging and weaving between spectators, then bounding up the steps two at a time. Kara thundered behind her.

"Slow down!" a woman yelled. She held out an arm to stop them, but the two girls pushed past her. At the top of the bleachers, they turned around. Eyes scanned the throng.

"Do you see him?" Jani panted.

"Not yet."

"But look, over there, next to that doorway. A security guard." Jani pointed to the gray uniformed man at the far entrance. "He'll help us."

"Let's go." They raced down the stairs.

"I'm getting tired of you girls galloping past. Now you…" The woman's voice was lost in the general hubbub as they reached the bottom of the stairs. Jani barely resisted the urge to turn and stick out her tongue at the bossy woman.

The security guard was still at the door when they arrived, out of breath and overheated. "Excuse me, sir," Jani gasped. "You have to help us."

The security guard looked at her with the most bored expression Jani had ever seen. Obviously, he was not a horse lover.

"We're looking for Officer Hughes," added Kara. "He's helping us find some stolen horses."

The guard perked up. "Stolen horses, you say?"

"Yes, and we just found one outside," Jani continued. "My friend, Penny, and my dad are stopping the thief and they sent us to find..."

"Show me where." The guard's hand on her arm stopped Jani from rushing off. "No, not back through the crowd. Out this door."

Moments later, they were outside the sale barn, away from the noise and din. Jani almost sighed with relief. She hated crowds. Beside her Kara inhaled deeply and Jani smiled. Apparently Kara did too.

A stable row filled with horses waiting for the sale ring stood before them. A few people loitered about with brushes, ropes, and saddles. "They're this way," said Jani, and ran. Horses and people looked at her curiously as she raced by.

She burst around a corner of the huge building with Kara and the security guard right behind her — to see Penny holding Sunny's lead rope and her dad talking calmly to the thief! Jani stopped to point them out to the security guard, and then followed the guard as he sauntered past her.

"What's happening here?" the guard said as he strode toward the three people and the horse.

The stranger quickly explained. He'd bought this horse, which he had no idea was stolen, before the sale started because he didn't want to take a chance on someone outbidding him in the sale ring. He was innocent, he said, completely innocent. *And* he wanted his money back.

Jani's dad turned to Kara. "Is he one of the men you saw?" he asked.

Kara shook her head.

"You saw the thieves?" asked the security guard, then his forehead wrinkled in concern. "Will they recognize you?"

"They didn't see me."

"Can you describe them?"

Without hesitation, Kara described the thieves again. Jani smiled. Kara was opening up, becoming less shy by the moment, it seemed. She was like a different person from the scared girl who'd talked to Officer Hughes just yesterday. Freedom and Whisper had been very good for her.

"Glad to see you all made it," came a voice from behind them. Jani looked back to see Officer Hughes striding toward them, a frown on his face. "But I have some bad news. I've checked the grounds and didn't see the stolen horses."

"That's because they're in disguise," said Penny. "This is Sunny, my horse. They dyed his mane and tail black and his white socks too, so that he looks like a buckskin."

A relieved smile leapt onto Officer Hughes face. "Good work, Penny."

Penny grinned. "It wouldn't matter if they dyed him pink and purple. I'd recognize my Sunny anywhere."

"Of course, it helped that when he saw you, he starting neighing and jumping around," added Jani's dad.

Penny laughed. "That's my Sunny boy! He saw me and wanted his treat." She pulled a cookie from her pocket and held it out to Sunny, who took it gently from her fingers.

"Thieves exposed by cookie loving horse," said Jani's dad. "What a great headline."

While Officer Hughes talked to the man who bought Sunny from the thieves, Jani went to the palomino's side and gave him a quick hug. "You want to keep looking, Penny?" she asked after pulling away. Her fingers tried to run through Sunny's colored mane, but caught in the dark hair. His mane was snarled and tangled.

"I can if you really want me to," her friend answered. "But…"

Jani nodded. "That's okay. If it were Keeta or Freedom I wouldn't want them out of my sight either. Kara and I will keep looking."

"Yeah, let's go," said Kara. There wasn't a flicker of hesitation in her eyes. She really was getting braver.

They searched all the corrals and Kara found two chestnuts that she thought *might* be the ones stolen, but she wasn't sure. She didn't know enough about horses to recognize them by their breed or build, and neither had any striking markings. She couldn't identify the bay at all, which was understandable. There was a horde of bays at the sale this year and even Jani had a hard time telling some of them apart. Of the gray Mystic and Whisper's pinto dam they saw no sign.

They started wandering the stable rows, one by one. "Do you think they sold all the stolen horses before the sale, like they tried with Sunny?" Kara asked dejectedly. She peered into the stalls on one side of the open aisle, while Jani checked the other side.

"I hope not. Poor Whisper. I'd feel so bad for him if his dam was gone."

"Me too," said Kara, and she sounded like she meant it.

"Kara?"

"Yeah?"

"You seem different."

"Really?" Kara glanced sideways at her. "I feel different — ever since I accepted that Whisper needed to go back to his mom. I didn't think I could let him go, but somehow I did. And giving him up so he could be happy and healthy changed something inside me." She looked at Jani sheepishly. "I know it sounds crazy. Sorry."

"No, it doesn't. I totally understand. Freedom taught me the same thing last year."

"Really? How?" asked Kara.

They reached the end of the stable row. "It's a long story. I'll tell you later, when we have more time, okay?"

"Sure."

They walked into the last aisle. It was deserted. No one was keeping their horses this far from the sale barn. Jani turned. Maybe they should check out the crowd from the bleachers again.

"Jani."

Jani turned back. "What is it? Do you see something?"

Kara nodded. Pointed. "Those two stall doors. They're closed both top and bottom."

A quiet thud came from the secured stall nearest them.

"It's them," whispered Kara, backing a step, her new bravery instantly gone. "I can feel it. I just know it's them."

Freedom snorted and tossed her ebony mane. Something was happening. She could feel it in her body, in her bones. The lost one was in danger.

Freedom trotted to the fence and neighed loudly, though she knew the lost one was too far away to hear her.

Mom came out of the house, looked around the backyard, and approached Freedom. Her hands felt light and soft on Freedom's neck, and yet so strong.

"Don't worry, girl," Mom said. "Little Whisper's owners are on their way and soon he'll be reunited with his mother."

Freedom snuffled her arm. How could she tell Mom what was wrong? She couldn't.

But there was still hope. The lost one was with Jani, and her girl was smart. If Jani was able, she would save her.

Kara followed Jani toward the stalls, slowly and silently. Jani peeked through a crack in the wall of the first stall, then stepped aside to let Kara look.

Kara peered into the darkness of the stall to see a black and white pinto mare. This horse had more black on it than Whisper's mother, but the thieves might have made more spots on her using the same dye they'd used on Sunny. She pulled back and nodded to the question in Jani's eyes. Yes, this could be one of the stolen horses.

The rustle of straw came from the neighboring stall, then a human growl telling a horse to hold still. Kara stiffened. Was the thief in the stall beside them with another of the stolen horses? Silently, Jani moved on to the second stall and peered inside.

Icy needles prickled the back of Kara's neck and she looked back the way they'd come. No one was there. She was being silly. No one was watching them. Jani touched her arm and she almost gasped aloud. Jani looked at her with wide eyes and motioned back the way they'd come, then Kara followed her away from the two stalls on stealthy feet.

"What did you see?" she whispered as soon as they were around the corner of the stable block.

"An older guy, blacking Mystic's hooves. I'm sure it was her, even though she's not gray anymore. She's a weird grayish red roan color."

Kara leaned back against the rough boards. Her teeth chattered for a moment, then she clenched her jaw tight. "I felt so weird back there. Like someone was watching us."

"He scares me too." Jani moved to peer around the corner, then retreated again. "One of us needs to go get Officer Hughes." She hesitated for a moment before continuing. "And one of us should stay here, in case he leaves. That way we'll know which way to go after him."

Kara swallowed and closed her eyes. After her attempt to keep Whisper, she had to atone somehow. And there was only one way she could think to do it. "I'll stay here," she said quickly, before she could change her mind.

"Are you sure?"

"Yes. But hurry." A shiver started at the base of her spine and traveled upward and outward.

"I will. I promise."

Kara opened her eyes in time to see Jani run toward the sale barn. Her gaze darted right and then left again. She was alone, completely alone, except for the thief, just yards away. Hopefully, he'd stay busy inside the stall for a few more minutes. That's all they'd need. Five minutes, max.

She stopped breathing as a chill swept over her. She could almost feel cold unfriendly eyes drilling into her head. Extreme dislike touching her. And something was coming closer. Something terrible.

I'm being stupid, she told herself, vehemently. *Nothing's coming. The thief doesn't even know I'm here. And even if he did, he doesn't know I saw him yesterday. I'm just another kid to him.*

But logical thoughts made no difference. Shivers prickled the back of her neck and lifted the hair on her arms. Was he coming closer? Sneaking up on her? She peered around the corner. The stall door was still shut.

Someone was behind her! She spun around.

Everything looked as it should. Some people walked toward her, then detoured down a stable aisle nearer the sale barn. She could hear the distant hubbub of the crowd, and pressed her back against the rough wall, closed her eyes again. She had to get a grip. Now wasn't the time to get overly imaginative.

"Hey, Dad?" A soft knock. Kara stopped breathing.

Hinges creaked. "Yep. I'm almost done. Come have a look."

Kara exhaled slowly. The thieves sounded so normal, even kindly toward each other.

"There's a guy interested in the bay thoroughbred," the son said. "He looks rich too. You want to go talk to him?"

"Sure. You can finish here. There's just one hoof left to black."

Kara launched herself from the wall of the stable. She had to keep the thieves together. If they split up, the police might never find them both. And Kara could think of only one way to stop the older man from leaving.

With trembling limbs, she walked around the corner.

Both men looked at her, then at each other. Their faces gave nothing away. A red roan mare stood between them, her eyes slightly alarmed.

More than anything, Kara wanted to turn and run. *They don't know who I am,* she reminded herself desperately. *I have to do this, for Whisper.*

Somehow she smiled at the two thieves. "She's pretty," Kara said, and then cleared her throat, hoping to control the tremor in her voice. "Are you selling her? My mom's buying me a horse today."

The younger man smiled. "Of course, she's for sale," his voice mellow and welcoming. "What kind of horse are you looking for?"

Kara tried her hardest to stand straight and tall in front of the two adults. If she acted confident enough, maybe they'd think the tremble in her voice was the way she always spoke. "Just the kind you ride."

"Trail riding? Jumping?"

"Uh, trails." She reached out to touch the reddish hair and the mare sniffed at her arm. "What's her name?"

"It's whatever you want it to be, sweetheart," said the older man, and grinned.

"I'll go look after the bay, Dad," said the son. He turned to leave.

"What I really hope to find is a horse with spots," Kara added quickly. "Do you have one with spots?"

"Wait a sec, Allan," the older man said. His son was already halfway down the aisle. "Before you go, show the young lady the other mare."

Allan walked back to them and slipped inside the

second stall, closing the door behind him. "Hold still, you," he muttered. Whisper's mother neighed loudly, and struck the wall.

"She's a great trail horse," the older man said, his voice oily smooth. "She just hates crowds."

"That's why you have them so far from the sale barn?" Kara asked innocently.

The man was about to answer when his eyes jerked behind Kara. Help had arrived!

"Got her," Allan said from inside the closed stall. The stall door swung open. He was ready to lead the horse out!

Kara threw her entire weight against the stall door. It slammed back and she heard the mare neigh in fear and anger, then Allan's exclamation of rage. Before he could push the door open again, Kara shot the bolt home.

"You little brat!"

Kara looked up to see the older man reaching for her. She cried out and recoiled.

"Police! Stop!"

For a moment, the man hesitated. And then he was running. Mystic exploded into a trot behind him, her step high and supple. The lead rope lashed between her front legs like a snake, and she blasted out a loud, rolling snort.

Officer Hughes flashed past Kara. But the thief was almost to the end of the aisle now. He was faster than Officer Hughes — he was going to escape!

Suddenly, Mystic leapt into a gallop, thundered past the thief, and launched her heels into the air! The thief threw himself backward to avoid being kicked, and fell onto his bottom.

"Hold still now. You are under arrest," said Officer Hughes as he grabbed the man.

A crashing noise came from beside Kara. Whisper's mother was kicking the stall again.

Jani reached her side, breathing heavily.

"Did you see that?" asked Kara. "Mystic helped Officer Hughes catch one of the thieves."

The pinto horse kicked the stall again.

"I saw! Cool!"

Another crashing sound from the stall, and a yell.

"She's mad at him for taking her baby away," said Jani. "*I* wouldn't want to be in there right now."

Apparently, Allan agreed. "I confess!" he yelled. "I helped steal the horses! Now just get me out of here. Please!"

Jani and Kara couldn't help but burst into laughter.

Jani and Penny were in high spirits all the way home. With Sunny and Mystic safe in the horse trailer behind them, the other stolen horses being transported to their homes by a professional hauler, and the thieves on their way to jail, they could finally relax.

As Jani embellished the story of how Kara acted like a buyer to delay the thieves, Kara sat silently, staring out the window. She perked up a bit when Jani told her dad and Penny about how Mystic and Whisper's mother did their part to help catch the thieves.

"Kara, you tell us the story now," said Jani's dad. "We obviously can't believe Jani's version."

"But they did, Dad! I promise," argued Jani.

"I'm just teasing you," he explained. "But I would like to hear Kara tell the story too."

"There's nothing more to tell, except it was pretty scary," Kara said, then added quietly, "And I had to do it. Whisper needs his mother."

"Very clear thinking, Kara," encouraged Jani's dad.

"Thanks," Kara said, and stared out the window, her face white.

What's wrong? Penny mouthed to Jani. Jani shrugged in response.

When they reached the outskirts of Red River, Jani's dad slowed the truck and trailer at the road that led to Kara's driveway. Jani noticed the girl stiffen beside her.

"Kara's mom isn't expecting her home until this evening," she said quickly to her dad. "Can she come with us to deliver the horses first?" She looked at Kara. "And then back to our house. Whisper might still be there."

A spark of hope lit Kara's face.

"What did Officer Hughes want to talk to you about, just before we left, Kara?" asked Jani's dad.

"Nothing."

"Nothing?"

"He asked where me and my mom moved from. He said it was for his report."

"He didn't ask *me* where *I* came from," said Penny, sounding injured.

"You've lived in Red River your whole life," laughed Jani. "That's why."

"Where did you move from?" Jani's dad asked Kara.

"Ontario," said Kara, her voice not inviting further questions.

"Well, that's a lot more interesting than being from here," Penny admitted.

They unloaded the horses at Mr. Regan's stable. Jani led Mystic into the barn beside Penny and Sunny.

"I'm going to stay for a while," said Penny. She flipped Sunny's mane. "I want to see if this black gunk will wash out."

"Come over as soon as you can," said Jani. "We need

134

to figure out this Kara thing. I don't really want her to go home to her freaky mom."

"But we can't tell anyone. We promised."

"I know." Jani shut the stall door behind Mystic, then leaned over the half door to slip the halter from the mare's head. "But there has to be some way we can help her." The mare sighed deeply and pulled a mouthful of hay from her full hay net. She was obviously happy to be home.

"I'll come soon," Penny promised.

When they reached Jani's home, Jani and Kara hurried around the side of the house. Keeta and Freedom were grazing in the lush pasture. "Keeta! Freedom!" Jani called. Both horses looked up, and Freedom neighed loudly. The two ambled to the fence, and thrust their heads over to be petted.

"Hey, Jani?" Kara's voice was almost a whisper.

"Yeah?"

Kara ran her fingers down Keeta's blazed face. "Do you mind if I go by myself? To the barn, I mean. To see if… he's still there?"

Jani looked at her new friend. "Are you sure?"

Kara nodded.

"Okay. I'll go in and tell mom about your daring horse rescue."

A small smile touched Kara's face. "In vivid detail, no doubt."

Jani laughed, hoping she didn't sound too strained. What was she going to do about Kara?

Kara waited until Jani was inside the house before she climbed through the fence. She gave Keeta and Freedom a quick hug each, then faced the barn. Was Whisper inside? How would she manage if he wasn't?

"Just go," she murmured to herself, then started to walk. She could hear the soft tread of a horse behind her, glanced back and smiled. Freedom was following her.

Kara pulled the barn door open and paused, took a deep breath, then strode toward the stall where she'd left Whisper that morning.

The stall was empty.

"Oh, Whisper," she murmured, and numbly opened the stall door. She wandered inside and knelt to put her hand on the small hollow in the straw. This was where he'd rested. And right beside it, the hollow she herself had made as she slept beside him. This was all she had left. She would never see her beloved Whisper again. Tears stung her eyes, and she let them slide down her cheeks without brushing them away.

At least he's back with his mother, she told herself fiercely. *That's the important thing. He'll have a happy, healthy life, even if it is with someone else.*

She heard the stall door open and Freedom's

concerned nicker, then felt the velvet muzzle on her shoulder. Shakily, she climbed to her feet and threw her arms around the ebony neck, buried her tear-streaked face in the black mane. The filly nuzzled her back as she cried out her heartbreak.

Sudden icy needles prickled the back of Kara's neck. Just like at the sale. But the thieves couldn't be here. They were in jail.

Freedom's loud neigh shattered the peace, and Kara looked up.

Her mom was striding toward them, her expression murderous.

"Kara, get over here right now! The car's packed. We're leaving!"

Kara fought her automatic response to obey. If she went with her mom, she'd never see Freedom or Jani or Penny again! She had to refuse to go. But the words wouldn't come.

Her mom's mouth twisted into a false smile. "No more playing games. You led me on a merry chase, my dear. That won't be happening again! Now, get over here." She stopped and waited.

"I… I don't want to leave."

Her mom's eyes narrowed. "What?"

"I don't want to leave," Kara said a little louder, a little braver.

"She got to you, didn't she?" The words were said slowly, as if each were its own sentence.

"Who?"

"You know who."

"Mom, you're not thinking straight."

"You're just like her, so don't call me Mom!" The phony smile became a sharp red line on Sandra's face.

"I'm sorry," Kara whimpered. She recoiled, and pressed against the back of the stall. Her mom had never hit her, but she'd *never* looked at Kara this way before. "I don't even know who Marjorie…"

"See? You know her! You know her name, so you must know her!" With anger-fuelled energy, Sandra stomped toward the stall.

Kara couldn't help it. She screamed.

Freedom wheeled away from her and jumped through the open stall door.

"No! Don't go! Don't go!" Kara shrieked, then watched with open-mouthed astonishment as Freedom lunged toward her mom with ears back and teeth bared.

Jani sensed something was wrong — terribly wrong —
a half second before she heard Freedom's distant neigh.

"The barn," she gasped in the middle of the story
she'd been telling her mom. "Something's happening."

Freedom's scream came again, louder, and Jani bolted
toward the door.

"Dave!" she heard her mom call behind her. "Come
quick!"

Jani clattered down the back stairs to the lawn and ran.
The barn had never seemed so far away before. She could
see Keeta standing in the open doorway of the building,
staring inside with startled eyes.

Finally Jani reached Keeta's side, and then she was
through the barn door. She stopped, stunned at the scene
that met her eyes. Freedom was standing at the closed
door of one of the stalls, her ears back and her blue
eyes flashing fire. Kara was behind her, and in the stall,
cowering beneath Freedom's fierce gaze, was Kara's
mother.

Jani hurried to Kara's side. "Are you okay?"

Kara nodded, mute.

"What's happening?" said Jani's mom from the
doorway of the barn.

"Who's that?" asked her dad.

"Kara's mom."

"You stay away from her," the woman growled, and advanced with fists clenched. Jani and Kara automatically stepped back as Freedom stepped forward. One dark hoof lashed out at the wooden door between them and the woman's words turned into a whimper. She pressed back against the wall.

Jani's mom hurried to the girls, and put her arms around Kara. "Tell me what happened," she said, sounding horrified.

"She came to take me away." Kara's voice was shaking. "She hates me. My mom hates me."

"You ruined my life, Marjorie!" the woman shrieked to the ceiling.

"Who's Marjorie?" asked Jani's dad, beside them now.

Kara sobbed and tried to cover her ears. "I don't know," she cried. "This is all my fault."

"No, it's not," Jani objected vehemently. "Remember what you said about Freedom and Whisper. How they made you wonder if your Mom's just crazy? Well, she is." She glared at the woman in the stall with hard eyes.

"No, I drove her to it." Kara could hardly speak anymore. She looked at her mother with teary eyes. "Mom, I'm so sorry. I wish…" Then she dissolved into tears.

"You're not my daughter!" The woman's voice was livid with rage. "You're nothing but an ungrateful…"

"That's enough!" Jani's father said loudly, drowning out her voice. He moved to stand beside Freedom, as if somehow his body could block the words spewing from the crazed woman's mouth.

"But she's right." Everyone turned to look toward the door of the barn. A stranger stood there, a woman, and behind her, Officer Hughes. The officer patted Keeta on the side, then squeezed past her into the barn.

An unearthly wail came from the stall, and Kara's mom slowly sank to the floor. Within seconds, Officer Hughes was in the stall beside her.

The strange woman knelt beside Kara. "My name is Ellie Thomas," she explained. "I work for Child Services, and I'm here to help you, Kara."

"Can you tell us what's happening here?" asked Jani's dad.

Ellie nodded. "But first, I need to speak to Kara alone. Is that okay, Kara?"

Kara looked up in shocked wonder as Officer Hughes led her mom past them to the barn door. Keeta stepped back, as if she didn't want the woman near her.

Sandra stopped. Looked back at Kara. For a moment, her expression softened, and she smiled. Then she looked up at Officer Hughes. "I'm glad it's finally over," she said, sounding completely sane for the first time. "She looks so much like Marjorie, that I kept forgetting."

"Let's go, Sandra," said Officer Hughes.

The woman nodded, then looked back at Kara one more time. "I'm sorry," she said simply. Then she turned and walked away, the police officer beside her.

A half hour later, when Kara and Ellie came out of the barn, one on each side of Freedom, Jani was waiting for them. She smiled as she remembered how the black filly had refused to leave the barn with the rest of them, and when Kara asked Ellie if she could stay, the social worker had reluctantly agreed. She'd obviously been unnerved by Freedom's display of aggression toward Kara's mother — but now the social worker's hand was on the ebony neck, her fingers playing in the thick mane. Freedom had won her over too.

Ellie touched Kara's shoulder when they reached Jani. "I'll go set up a place for you to stay tonight, Kara."

Kara nodded. "Thanks, Ellie."

When the social worker was halfway to the house, Kara whispered to Jani, "Is *she* gone?"

Jani nodded. "Officer Hughes took her away."

A shudder passed through Kara's body and she collapsed against Freedom's shoulder. "I never want to see her again. Ever."

"But…"

"She's not my mom, Jani," said Kara, her voice bubbling over with tentative happiness. "I'm a stolen kid. She hated my *real* mom, Marjorie. But my real mom

143

didn't know that. She thought Sandra was a friend. So when Sandra offered to baby-sit me one day, she said yes, and Sandra stole me."

"Wow."

"My real mom and dad love me. They've been searching for me for years. That's why she, Sandra, made us move all the time. Because Mom and Dad never gave up. They almost caught us a bunch of times, but Sandra would always run before they could get me back."

Jani was silent. What could she say? But she didn't need to say anything. Kara continued without any prompting.

"And that's not all. Ellie says that Sandra's unstable, and that as I got older and looked more like my mom, she became even crazier. That's why she started calling me Marjorie. It was like she was haunted by her guilt, or something like that."

"*Amazing.*"

"It is, isn't it?" Kara smiled, and for the first time since she'd met the girl, Jani could see it was a real smile. "And it's so cool to look like my real mom. It's like I don't even know them, but I know I belong with them. Weird, eh?"

Freedom nickered quietly and Kara hugged her around her neck. Jani's fingers trickled down the filly's nose.

"You know what else is weird?" asked Jani, glad she finally had something to say other than single word exclamations.

"What's that?"

"You wouldn't have ever found your real parents if you hadn't helped Whisper go back to his mom."

Kara's face turned pale, and when she spoke, her voice was almost inaudible. "And I almost didn't do it."

"But you did do it, and that's what matters. You did what you knew was right."

Kara nodded. "I did."

"So where do your parents live?" Jani's voice was hopeful. She already thought of Kara as a friend, and knew Penny did too.

A shadow crossed Kara's face. "Not even close to Red River."

"No."

"But I'll ask if we can come visit. I'd hate to never see you or Penny, Keeta or Sunny again. And I don't think I could live if I couldn't see Freedom."

"I know what you mean."

"I asked Ellie one favor and I hope its okay with you, and your mom and dad too."

"What?"

"I asked if I can meet my parents here, at your house."

"Of course, you can," said Jani. "That would be awesome."

Penny and Sunny arrived the next morning about fifteen minutes before Kara was to arrive. She dismounted the gelding by the pasture gate.

"Hi!" Jani called as she walked across the back lawn toward them. "Hey, he looks great. You got out most of the black."

Penny wrinkled her nose. "Well, I wouldn't say 'great'. It's still kind of gray, but it's a lot better than it was."

Jani gave the gelding a quick pat, and then pulled a horse treat from her pocket. "He's gorgeous, even with tinted mane." She laughed when Keeta reached across the fence and nudged her. "Yes, I have some for you too." She held out two horse treats in two hands, one each for Keeta and Freedom.

"Hey, Jani, I was wondering something."

"Yeah?"

"What do you think of me boarding Sunny here instead of at Mr. Regan's stable?"

"Great idea! That would be so awesome."

A relieved look crossed Penny's face. "I know," she added. "We always go riding together anyway, and you have two extra stalls. And no one will ever steal Sunny again with Freedom on duty." She stroked the black's face. "Right, girl?"

"They wouldn't dare," agreed Jani. "I'm sure Mom and Dad will agree. They like Sunny. And it'll look so pretty, black and gold and red spotted horses in the pasture."

"Keeta might even learn to like him."

"Well, I wouldn't count on that."

Sunny chose that moment to lean over the fence and touch Keeta's shoulder. The mare looked at him with contempt, laid her ears back, and stepped away from him. Both girls burst out laughing.

By the time Kara arrived, the three horses were tied side by side along the inside of the pasture fence.

"There's a rubber curry in the bucket there," said Jani, after they said their hellos. She noticed Kara's hand trembling as she picked up the rubber brush. And no wonder. Jani could only imagine how stressful it would be to see your mom and dad for the very first time in memory!

"You nervous?" asked Penny, bringing the obvious out into the open.

Kara nodded. "What if they don't like me?"

"Don't worry. They'll like you. You're very likeable, really," said Penny. Freedom nickered as if punctuating her words.

Kara smiled. "Thanks, guys. This is all because of you, you know. If you hadn't... well. I'd probably be halfway to Texas by now, not realizing that my *mom* was really my kidnapper."

"That's so freaky," said Penny.

"I bet you grow up to be a writer someday," said

147

Jani. "I heard someone say once that kids who have a rough time being a kid, have lots to write about when they're old."

Kara smiled. "Maybe that'll make it all worthwhile. Now that it's over. And as long as my real mom and dad love me."

"They will."

"We promise." This time both Keeta and Freedom nickered, then Sunny leaned toward Keeta and whinnied softly. "See? It's unanimous," added Jani. "They're going to adore you."

"And they'll want to make up for twelve years of not being able to spoil you."

"And if you have grandparents, well, watch out. You're going to be showered with presents."

Kara laughed out loud. "You guys can always make me feel better."

Suddenly, Freedom raised her head. Kara glanced toward the house and inhaled sharply. Her hand froze on Freedom's glistening side. "They're here."

The three adults, Ellie and the man and woman, walked slowly across the back lawn.

"Just keep brushing Freedom," Jani whispered over Keeta's back. "That always helps me when things are hard."

Kara nodded and her hand began to move again, tentatively at first, and then her strokes became stronger, firmer.

The adults stopped at the fence. Jani noticed that Kara's mom had tears on her face — and she did look a lot like Kara. They even had the same hairstyle. But best of all, both she and Kara's dad had kind faces. An almost overwhelming relief washed over Jani. Kara deserved these parents, good, kind people who would love her.

Ellie, the social worker, stood with them for a moment, then after a nod from Kara's dad, said she would return in a few minutes. As she walked away, Kara's mom spoke softly. "Hi, Kara."

Kara stopped brushing Freedom, and glanced at her mom shyly. "Hi," she whispered. Her gaze dropped to the ground, and then as if she suddenly remembered Jani's words, she continued to brush Freedom.

"We're so…" Kara's mom stopped speaking, overcome with emotion.

"We're so happy to finally see you," her dad finished, then added, "Sweetheart."

"And we're so sorry," her mom choked out. "We trusted Sandra."

"It wasn't your fault," said Kara, and started to cry. "You didn't know."

Kara's dad cleared his throat and put his arm around his wife's shoulders. "These are beautiful horses," he said, as if giving her time to recompose herself. "Do they belong to you girls?"

"The palomino is mine," said Penny. "His name's Sunny. My name is Penny, by the way."

"And the other two are mine. They're Freedom and Keeta. I'm Jani. We're Kara's friends from school."

"It's so nice to meet you girls," said Kara's mom, sounding a little less emotional. "We'll come back to visit, Kara. We promise."

Jani smiled. She like Kara's mom. She seemed more than just nice. She seemed compassionate, sympathetic, and gentle. "Do you want to help brush them?" she offered.

"I'd love to." Kara's mom slipped through the rail fence. "Just show me what to do."

Jani's gaze met Kara's across the horses' backs and an unspoken thought passed between them. "Kara can show you," said Jani. She handed Kara's mom her brush. "You can help her brush Freedom."

Kara swallowed nervously. "You move the brush like this, with the hair and not against it," she started, her voice quiet. "And that's a body brush so you don't push too hard. It helps to remove the dirt that gets down near her skin." Kara smiled when her mom tentatively stroked the brush along Freedom's opposite side.

"She has lovely eyes," Kara's mom said, and her gaze met Kara's across the Freedom's back.

"She saved me. More than once…" Kara paused. "…Mom."

Kara's mom blinked back tears.

"I'll tell you all about it, later, okay?" Kara looked at her dad. "I'll tell you both everything."

"Sounds wonderful, sweetheart," said Kara's dad, his voice quavering. "We want to hear everything you have to tell us. Absolutely everything."

For a moment, the whisk of brushes shining glossy coats was the only sound. Then Kara's dad spoke again. "I wish I had a camera so I could take a picture of you three girls brushing your three horses." His voice was stronger now. He was regaining his composure again. "It would be the perfect picture."

Behind Jani, Penny inhaled sharply, but Jani didn't need her friend to tell her what she was thinking. She could recognize an opportunity when she heard one.

"I know what would make the picture perfect for Kara," she said without hesitation.

Both Kara's parents turned toward her hopefully, and Jani could see the desire to please their daughter plain on their faces. They wanted to shower her with gifts and love and affection to make up for all the lost time.

"A horse of her own," interjected Penny.

"Yes," added Jani, and grinned. "A magical foal named Whisper."

"Magical, eh? Just like your Freedom? I think Kara might need a friend like that," said Kara's dad.

"In fact, I'm sure she does," added Kara's mom, and then she laughed aloud when Freedom neighed in agreement.

Freedom stepped back so Kara could duck beneath her neck, then sighed contentedly as the girl threw her arms around her mother, her real mother. Moments later, Kara's dad was over the fence and hugging them too.

Quietly, Jani and Penny unclipped the horses. Keeta wandered away to graze with Sunny close behind her, and Jani and Penny walked to the house. But Freedom didn't move.

She felt the swelling of Kara's heart, as the girl stood in the circle of her parents' arms, as if Kara's heart was inside her own chest. She felt Kara's healing, her acceptance, and finally, her belonging.

And then the feeling diminished. Not because Kara felt it any less — Freedom knew that — but because the unusual connection between girl and horse was ending. It was no longer necessary.

However, before the connection was completely gone, the girl looked over at her and smiled. She thought, *thank you,* to Freedom. Then, *I'll love you forever.*

Freedom nickered affectionately. She would miss this closeness with Kara — but she too would let go. The lost one didn't need her anymore. She had been found.